Penguin Books
Elegy for a Revolutio[n

C. J. Driver was born in Cape Town in 1939. He was educated at St Andrew's College, Grahamstown, and at the University of Cape Town, where he took various degrees, edited the student newspaper, and served on the Student Council. He was then elected President of the left-wing National Union of South African Students, and worked for it for two years, incurring the wrath of both the then Minister of Justice, Mr Vorster, and the leader of the official Opposition. He was detained for a short time in 1964, and many of his friends were involved in trials and long prison sentences. The South African Government refused to renew his passport in 1966.

In 1964 Driver came to England, where he taught for a year at Sevenoaks School, before going to Trinity College, Oxford, to read for a B.Phil. After two years there he married and returned to Sevenoaks School, where he is now housemaster of the International Sixth Form Centre.

In 1965 Driver began to write stories as well as the poems which were being occasionally published in magazines in England and South Africa. One of these stories he showed to Cyril Connolly, who told him it read like the start of a novel. It is now substantially Chapter 1 of *Elegy for a Revolutionary*. C. J. Driver has also contributed to the Penguin *South African Writing Today*, and his work is represented in *The Penguin Book of South African Verse*. A story, *False Impossible Shore*, will be published in *Penguin Modern Stories 8*.

C. J. Driver

Elegy for a Revolutionary

Penguin Books

Penguin Books Ltd, Harmondsworth,
Middlesex, England
Penguin Books Australia Ltd, Ringwood,
Victoria, Australia

First published by Faber & Faber 1969
Published in Penguin Books 1971

Made and printed in Great Britain by
Cox & Wyman Ltd, London, Reading and Fakenham
Set in Intertype Plantin

for Maeder Osler and Winston Nagan

No characters in this novel are intended to be actual people; and the various characters who are mentioned as holding this or that position do not refer to any actual holders of any of these positions.

Part One

The Bright-dancing Air

Prologue

Sometimes it seemed to Quick that he was haunted by them, those alive and those dead. It might happen at any moment of the day that the air would be crowded with their faces, this one unsmiling, this one laughing, this one seeming so sure of what he believed that nothing could shake his certainty, and this one in such despair that not even the terrible could hurt him any more; and, in that last, each face seemed to merge until it became only a dream of the daytime sky.

Each evening, when it was time for him to leave the library to go home, he would be almost afraid to go, since the faces might then resolve themselves into no more than images, the terrors and the love which bound this part of his mind to that. What his real life was he knew – it was in his house, with his wife and daughter, in his books and his work; but his life, as it was in his mind, had ended four years before, so that now he doubted even his own mind. So too, he would wonder whether these others, those who like him survived by luck or planning or cunning or treachery, had the same sense of death. Did they wake every morning to count the years and the months, forward to the time of release and backward to the time of the betrayal? Or did they wake to look at the bright-dancing air for the heart of the dead ones?

Not knowing the answer, for himself or for anyone else, he would re-create the deaths and the betrayals again and again, looking for the one moment when the pattern had changed, when the choices he had made turned themselves inside out and when the one crucial choice said, You made me a long time ago – don't you remember? He could never remember well enough and so, again and again, he would force the choices to present themselves again. That was where it ended, that was where it began, he would think – and then he would change his mind and would work out the series again, as if the incidents and the people were numbers which could be shuffled like playing-cards to give a new advantage to the man who held the bank.

I

From the beginning the organization had been planned so that, when emergencies arose, they could be swiftly and efficiently dealt with. At the first proper meeting of the national committee, the three men present had decided that an organization of its nature could be expected to stay alive for a maximum of two years; so, they had agreed, regional groups should be instructed to plan what should be done when members of the organization started to be arrested by the Security police. In fact, partly because other emergencies arose so often and partly because the organization was so efficient that it had lasted nearly twice as long as the maximum planned for, the regional groups never got around to deciding what should be done when the end came.

For Hunter, who was trained to note times exactly, the final emergency started at thirteen minutes to ten. He had been home only ten minutes then and, even though he was lying on his bed, was still dressed; he had already checked, as he did every night when he came back to his flat, no matter how late it was, that nothing had been moved from the position which he had determined for it. At the fourth ring, he picked up the phone and said simply, 'Hullo.'

'Hunter?'

'Yes.' He did not bother to ask who was speaking.

'I'm afraid things are breaking up. Someone was arrested in Johannesburg about two hours ago and that makes things pretty much at an end.' Hunter said, 'Thank you for telling me,' and put the phone down. He did not move immediately but sat on the edge of his bed. Then he went to his wardrobe, took from it a kit-bag, and packed into it his suit jacket, two shirts, two tee-shirts, three pairs of underpants, five pairs of socks, ten handkerchiefs, a pair of slacks, a towel, and a pair of black shoes. He dumped the kit-bag on his bed and pulled the top drawer of his dressing-table right out and put it on the bed next to the kit-bag. From the drawer he took an envelope which he opened. He took the fifteen five-pound notes and the twenty-five singles which it contained and put them in his back pocket. Then he took a wallet from the drawer and took from it his passport and driving licence. These he put in his shirt pocket. He turned the drawer over on his bed and carefully tore from the bottom five sheets of paper which had been taped to it. These he burnt very carefully, holding each sheet over the metal waste-paper bin so that the ashes would not fall on the floor. Then he put the drawer back in the dressing-table and replaced the rest of its contents before closing it.

He took the waste-paper bin into the bathroom and swilled the ash down the lavatory. When the last trace was flushed away, he took the bin into the kitchen and washed it out. Still carrying the bin, he collected three apples, three oranges, and two bars of chocolate from the food cupboard and took these and the waste-paper bin back to his bedroom. The food he put in the top of the kit-bag. He then changed his trousers for his suit trousers, pulled on a heavy black polo-neck sweater and changed his thin shoes for a pair of stout boots with rubber soles and heels. Lastly, he took a navy-blue duffle coat from behind the bedroom door and put it on.

He again stood still for a moment or two, checking that he had forgotten nothing. He then went back to the kitchen, turning out the light as he did so. Looking out of the kitchen window, he could not see anybody standing at the back of the building. He went into the dark sitting-room. Again he looked out of the window and again could not see anybody. He went back to his bedroom and wrote on a piece of writing paper, AWAY FOR TWO DAYS. BACK SATURDAY. PLEASE TAKE DIRTY WASHING FROM BEHIND DOOR. This note he left lying on his pillow – although he did not have a servant, the police, if they searched his flat, might find the note and expect him back. As well, if they searched his flat, they might waste some time looking for a servant who did not exist. Lastly, he turned out the light at the door, although he had left the reading lamp next to his bed burning.

He went into the kitchen again, opened the window, hitched his kit-bag over his shoulder, climbed out on to the fire escape, and pulled the window shut behind him. It was only one flight down to the ground. Although he did not expect to find anyone watching the front of the building, for even the members of his group did not know his address and only one had known his phone number, he did not go towards his car at the front of the building but left the block of flats by the rear entrance. Just before the road he stopped in the shadows. He had practised this far seven times one week three months before. He looked at his watch and saw that he had managed to do this part of the operation in nine minutes, a minute faster than he had managed in practice.

The next part of the operation he had not tried. So, before starting, he rehearsed his movements for the next half hour.

He would walk to Patricia's flat. That should take twenty minutes. If by chance she was not in, he would let himself in with the key she had given him and would wait for her. But most week nights she was in bed by ten-thirty. He must remember to leave his bag in the foyer of her block of flats – it would be better to take the risk of having it stolen than to let her see it.

If she noticed his dress, she might comment. He would say that he had been down to the docks to talk to the fishermen. If the police questioned her after he had gone, they might think that he was planning to try that way. She would probably not notice.

He would ask to borrow her car – he had done that before when he did not want to use his own. He would promise to return it by the next evening; she did not use the car during the day and so would not object. If by any chance she did, he knew that he would be able to persuade her.

He would leave, not by a main road, but by a series of side roads. There was unlikely to be a road block on the main road north so soon but there might be one close to town. Even if he were stopped by a road block, it would probably not be intended for him; if it was, there was a chance that the police might be hoping to identify him by his car.

With any luck, he would be at the border before dawn. Six hours in Patricia's fast little car would be easy.

Here he was reaching a stage which he had practised already. One week-end, about four months before, and without informing the other members of the group, he had driven his car to the border. Letting down a tyre as though he had had to abandon the car after a puncture – this time he must remember to let down the spare tyre too – he had left the car about five miles short of the border post and had cut across country so that he would miss it by about five miles. He had gone as far as he could in five hours – this, he knew, must take him well into Bechuanaland – and then retraced his steps; on his way back he had done a double check of the landmarks. He had chosen a night when there was a full moon; this time it would be more difficult but he should be able to spot his way. When he reached his car again, he had not seen anyone for eleven hours. He had pumped up the tyre, turned the car round, driven for a few miles, slept in the car for three hours, and had then driven back to town. This time he would do exactly the same, except that he would not come back. He could, he knew, probably use his passport to cross at the border-post; if he got that far it would be unlikely that the police were looking for him yet. But he preferred not to use his passport.

He did not like leaving the shadows at the back of the block of flats but he knew that, if he snaked along the pavement to Patricia's flat, he might attract the attention of a patrolling police van. He slipped the kit-bag off his shoulder and walked off as fast but as casually as possible, swinging the bag. So far so good, he thought.

Raymond Roseman's escape was less well-planned but, as it happened, equally effective. He arrived home, about half an hour after the time that Hunter had reached his flat, and found his wife waiting for him. 'Someone's been phoning you every ten minutes,' she said. 'I don't know who it is – he won't give his name or say why he wants you. He rings off now if I answer the phone. I was beginning to get worried.'

'I wonder who it is. I think I'd better go out for a moment or two and ring from the corner – if I'm away longer than five minutes it means that I've had to go out for a while. But I should be back by midnight at the latest.'

Mrs Roseman didn't ask any questions; her husband had been active in politics ever since she had known him and, although she agreed with all his opinions, she did not want to know too much about his actions. She was used to his disappearing to what she supposed were meetings at any time of the night and knew that he was going to phone from the call-box and not from their own phone because they thought theirs was tapped. But she would not go to bed until he came in – sometimes when he did he liked to talk to her. Roseman made two calls from the call box. The first was to Arthur Devis; there was no reply. The second was to Stevens – he was meant to do this in emergencies only and might have trouble if this was not one. The phone was answered immediately; 'Hullo,' he said, 'may I speak to Stevens?'

'Stevens here.'

'This is Raymond. Have you been trying to phone me?'

'Yes. Where are you phoning from?'

'A call-box.'

'The usual one?'

'Yes.'

'Can you meet me on the beach-front in ten minutes?'

'Of course.'

Roseman and Stevens lived only a mile apart and they often met half-way between their homes, down on the beach-front. They would stroll along the front, from opposite directions, and stop to talk as if they had met casually; at night, with only a few people around, and in the open air, there seemed little chance of the meeting being noticed.

When they met, Stevens took Roseman by the arm and together they walked down the front. 'I have bad news, I'm afraid. Charlie de Klerk was arrested in Johannesburg earlier this evening – the police found a lot of material in his car. He must have been in the process of transporting it.'

'Oh my God!' De Klerk was the organization's chief source of explosives, getting them from some place in the Transvaal and transporting them to the various regional groups; he wasn't meant to know more than one person in each group but as the organization had grown so he had come to know more and more people – only the national committee knew as many members as De Klerk did. It did not matter that more than one person knew De Klerk – it was a form of insurance against his betraying them to the police for more money than they gave him for the explosives. De Klerk had the best cover possible, for he supplied the explosives for money only; the members of the organization had always known, however, that if the police got on to Charlie, he would talk almost immediately. But there had seemed no other way of getting the explosives.

'Did the Johannesburg people tell you?' asked Roseman.

'Yes.'

'What are they doing?'

'The people who Charlie knew have moved out already. I gather that they are trying to get the people from the other places to do that too.'

'What about Arthur and the rest?'

'I have reached Hunter myself. Nobody seems to be able to get Devis. Quick's trying to get him and Jeremy.'

'Shall I do something?'

'No. If Quick doesn't get them by midnight, I'll try myself. You'd better try to get away.'

'What about you?'

'I should be all right. Charlie doesn't know any of the national people.' Roseman realized what he hadn't realized before – Stevens must be on the national committee, he thought; but he did not draw attention to the mistake. Stevens went on, 'Even if the police get Quick, he doesn't know anything more than vague details. And Jeremy's all right, of course. I'm not sure about Arthur.'

So Stevens thinks that Arthur might talk, thought Roseman; he was perhaps right. 'Would Hunter give you away?' he asked.

'I'm willing to bet the police won't get Hunter; even if they did, he wouldn't talk. What about you, Raymond? Would you talk?' When he asked that question, Roseman wondered, suddenly, whether he had made the mistake about the national committee deliberately. He did not reply for a long time, and, when he did, he spoke very quietly; 'I wish I could say that I would never talk, Ian. But I don't know – I wouldn't talk easily or quickly but they could break me.'

'That's why I think you should go.'

'I'm sorry,' and Roseman meant not that he was sorry that he had to go but that he was sorry for his limitation of strength.

'Don't be sorry – you've already proved yourself and now it's time for you to go. There are two hundred pounds in this envelope; you'll need it and your wife will need what you've got saved when they come to join you. Here, take it. We won't be needing it much longer.'

'Thank you.' Roseman looked at Stevens – his face was hard to see in the beach-front lights; dark eyes and shadows, line and angle, indefinite definition. As Roseman watched, he turned away and rested his arms on the sea-wall, almost as if he were praying to the sea; then he ran his hands over the stone, backwards and forwards, testing its reality by touch.

'What will you do now?' asked Roseman.

'Even if I knew I would not tell you.' Suddenly Stevens was decisive again. 'You must go now, immediately, and you will not tell me how, will you? The organization is finished; you owe it nothing, not even money. Good-bye, boy, and look after yourself.'

'Shall I let you know when I'm safe?'

'No. You are not to get in touch with me again. I'll hear from the police if you don't make it.'

'I wouldn't talk, Ian; you know?'

'Yes, I know, boy. Good-bye,' said Stevens and turned away into the dark. Roseman looked after him for a moment, then looked at his watch, and turned and walked quickly down the front.

Roseman was back home within ten minutes. His wife was sitting in the drawing-room, not doing anything. He went over and sat on the arm of her chair but did not touch her.

'Sweetheart, I'm afraid there's trouble. I shall have to go off tonight and I won't be back for some time' – he looked at his watch; it was nearly eleven – 'and I shall have to leave in five minutes' time.'

'How serious is it, Ray? Is it the police?'

'They'll probably come to question you in a day or two, though I hope they won't come tonight. They may not come for a week even. But I'm fairly sure they'll come.'

'And you won't be here?'

'No, I can't be here. You don't want me to explain, do you?'

'No. If the police come I want to be able not to lie, just to be able to say that you've gone and that I don't know where or why.'

'It won't be for long, darling. It shouldn't be more than a couple of months. I'll write and tell you what to do.'

'Will you let me know when you're safe?'

'I'll send you a cable.'

She leaned her head against his arm for a moment. Then she got up and said, 'Well, shall I pack you a case? Is there anything that you particularly need? What about money?'

'Money is all right. You'll have enough in the bank for you and the kids, won't you, for a couple of months?'

'Yes, we'll manage. Come upstairs and tell me what you want me to pack.'

'I have a couple of things to do first down here. Will you just pack the usual sort of things?' She didn't answer but left him standing there. As soon as she had gone, he went to the bookshelf next to his desk and, choosing one of the volumes, took from between its pages an envelope. This he took to the fireplace and burnt. As he was doing so, some of the ash blew on to the carpet – he tried to pick the ash up but could not, so scuffed it into the carpet. Then he went back to his desk and took from a top drawer his passport. He slipped this into his inside pocket next to the envelope which Stevens had given him. Then he took his brief-case and loaded into it a selection of books from the shelf and some of the papers from his desk.

By the time he was finished, his wife was downstairs again, carrying a small suitcase. 'I haven't put much in it, dear,' she said. 'I thought that you wouldn't want to be cluttered.'

'Thank you, darling. I'll have to take the car. I'll let you know tomorrow or the next day where you'll be able to find it. You haven't lost your keys, have you?' She shook her head. 'Oh, and darling, will you tell the office if they phone that you don't know where I am? Just that, nothing more. I'll do the rest in due course.'

They said good-bye very quickly, neither daring to look at the other's face for more than a moment and each surprising the other with the dryness of their mouths when they kissed. She had closed the front door before he was in the car.

He had decided, as he was walking back from meeting Stevens, to abandon his original plan of escape which had been to cross the border into Bechuanaland, much as Hunter had planned. He had no reason for adopting a new plan, particularly since it was less likely to succeed than the more obvious one. But it seemed somehow to fit in – why, he did not completely know. He would go by air, leaving the car at the airport and catching the midnight flight to Johannesburg. He had done the flight before, several times, and knew that it was always full, so, if necessary, he would lie to the booking-clerk that his mother was desperately ill; he knew that most airlines would help someone in an emergency. Once he was in Johannesburg, he would get on the first flight he could to Nairobi or Lusaka, or even if necessary Salisbury – there should be early morning flights not fully booked. He would use his passport quite normally. With any luck he'd be out of the country by the next morning.

The police might be waiting at the airport. They might check on all flights to Johannesburg and become suspicious when they recognized his name. They might be waiting for him in Johannesburg. They might catch him at the passport desk. He might not be able to get a plane out of the country. But it seemed necessary to try that way. He might even make it, given a little luck. It was going to be a long night, all the same.

Arthur Devis did not escape. Five Security policemen arrested him at his flat at just after eleven-thirty.

It was, in many ways, very funny. Arthur and his flat-mate, Henry Naude, and two of their girl-friends had spent the evening drinking in a bar near Muizenberg, for they had gone swimming in the afternoon. When the bar had closed at ten-thirty, they had all been drunk enough to want to go on drinking. So they had decided to call in at the home of one of Henry's friends and persuade him to join them and to buy some brandy from a shebeen; Koos Reisman was coloured and so was able to go to shebeens where white men were not welcomed. All this they did and by eleven-thirty they were back in the flat with two bottles of brandy.

Arthur did not realize that the Security police had arrived until he heard Henry at the front door saying, as loudly as he could to warn the others, 'May I see your credentials, please?' He stood up, not looking at the others, and went into the hall. There were three plain clothes policemen standing in the doorway; he knew the man in front, Sergeant van der Post. He had been questioned by him once before, at a student demonstration which had got out of hand; now he was drunk enough not to care. 'Kom binne, Sersant,' he shouted raucously. 'Daar is brandewyn hier.' The sergeant said nothing for about ten seconds and then, 'Mr Devis, we have come to search your flat and we are then taking you into detention for questioning.' Arthur didn't bother to ask for the search warrant – the police did not need one; anyway, he did not care if they searched the flat – he kept nothing there.

Just then there was a loud banging at the back door. Henry and Arthur went into the kitchen, followed by Sergeant van der Post. There were two men at the back door, trying to get into the flat. Arthur realized that they must have been sent to guard it in case he tried to make a getaway. The sergeant said to Henry, 'Open the door for them.'

'No,' replied Henry; 'I have lost the back door key.' It was perfectly true, Arthur knew – Henry lost most keys; even when he did not, he usually didn't bother to lock anything. The sergeant looked at him without replying, again for at least ten seconds – he had a trick of doing this. It gives you the impression that he does not think that anyone outside him exists as an object, thought Arthur; except as far as it conforms to an image which he has already formed. Arthur realized suddenly that the sergeant would be a very dangerous person if your behaviour did not conform to the image. It was dangerous but it could be used to rattle him – something to remember for later, Arthur thought. The sergeant said nothing to Henry but shouted to the other policemen, 'Come round the front entrance.' No sooner were they there than he told one to go back to the car and another to wait at the front entrance of the block of flats.

Then the searching started, one man to each bedroom, one doing the kitchen and bathroom. Arthur went into his bedroom which the sergeant was searching himself – he sat in his armchair so that he could watch. To watch the search, very slow, very careful, was impressive; whenever the sergeant came across anything that he thought might be interesting, he did not look at it immediately but put it on top of Arthur's desk. First he searched the desk, then the bookcase, taking each book out, looking at its title, checking that the book inside the dust covers was the right one, shaking it to see that nothing was concealed in its pages, and then replacing it. He's going to take hours, thought Arthur; I'm not going to sit here and watch him. He won't find anything – unless he searches me, when he'll find two letters from my mother and my passport, both in my jacket pocket. I wonder – I may be able to fool him. He stood up. 'Sergeant, I'm going to have a shave, if you have no objection; I use an electric razor so I won't cut my throat, just in case you care.' The sergeant stood up – again the long pause and the almost blind look; no, not blind, because he sees something. But it is as though what he sees is standing about three feet in front of me.

'You may shave, Mr Devis, but I want you to do it in here where I can watch you.'

'It's a good thing I don't want to go to the lavatory,' he replied; but the sergeant seemed not to hear him.

While Arthur was shaving, the policeman who was searching Henry's bedroom, which also served as the flat's sitting-room, came in and said, 'Sergeant, the little girl is crying – she wants to go home.' Again the long pause; good, thought Arthur, it's habit and not just a practice to be used on political suspects.

'She can go home. Take her name and address.'

'Yes, Sergeant.'

'Will it be all right if I drive her in your car, Arthur?' Henry asked from the doorway.

'Sure, Henry. Here the keys are,' he said, throwing them across the room.

'Just wait, Mr Naude,' said the Sergeant. 'When will you be back?'

'In ten minutes. I'll be back, don't you worry, Sergeant.' He was very angry, Arthur could hear – when he was, he used such a polite voice that you would think that he intended a compliment. He's probably mad about the girl's crying; no, perhaps not, he's too kind for that, he's probably just resenting having his room searched. I'm sorry for his girl – she couldn't have expected the whole bloody Security police to join in tonight too.

He was beginning to feel sober now – the shaving helped. He ran the razor once more over his face, then he put it away in his drawer. He took his jacket from the chair where he had thrown it when he started to shave and hung it over the back of the armchair between the desk and the bookcase, which the sergeant was still searching. Then he said to the sergeant, 'I'm going next door to talk to my girl. All right?'

Again the pause. 'No. I will ask her to come in here. I want you where I can see you.'

'I'm very flattered, Sergeant.'

The sergeant went to the doorway and called out, 'Miss, Mr Devis would like to speak to you in next door.' Miss? thought Arthur; so he doesn't know her name – I must remember not to use it. The girl followed the sergeant into the room and came to sit on the arm of Arthur's chair; she was very white, he noticed, but he was pleased that she tried to smile at him. She's a good girl, this, he thought, and he smiled back.

'Are you all right, honey?' he asked.

'Yes. Are you?' she said.

'I'm still a bit tight. Would you like to make some coffee? Perhaps the Security police would like some too. And Koos. How is he?'

'Koos says that he's used to this sort of thing – he's having a chat to the other policeman while he searches Henry's room.'

'What are they talking about?'

'Whether the policeman's son should do German or Latin for his Matric exams.'

'These schoolmasters. They're incredible.'

'I'll make some coffee. Would you like some?' She spoke to the sergeant. He looked up, did his non-stare at her, then nodded.

'I'll just ask the others too,' she said. Arthur, as he watched her leave the room, thought that it was a pity that it had to be tonight that this happened. It's funny that Koos should be talking to the police about exams – I expect they are planning to use the old trick on me in solitary: one man to be nasty and one man to be nice. That way the nice one pretends to protect you from the nasty, after a while you believe him because you've got nothing else to believe, and then he either persuades you to talk or you just tell him, because he's your friend. Oh no, not for me!

The sergeant had by now finished searching the bookcase and the wardrobe and had started on the dressing-table. Arthur stood up, very casually, and took his jacket from the back of his chair – he went over to the wardrobe and, as naturally and as noisily as possible, took out a hanger, on which he hung the jacket. This he put in the wardrobe and then slammed the door. The sergeant had looked up when he stood up but, when he saw what Arthur was doing, he had gone on with his search. Perhaps I've got away with it, Arthur thought; stupid man – what an obvious trick for me to play and he's not going to get it.

When the girl came back with the coffee, he took his mug and said, 'Will you ask Koos to bring some brandy in here? I want some in my coffee and the sergeant doesn't want me out of here.' Koos came in in a few moments, carrying a bottle. He addressed the sergeant first. 'Good evening, Sergeant van der Post.' Then he grinned at Arthur, came over, and poured a good tot of brandy into the mug. 'You'll be needing that, man,' and then he leaned over to whisper, 'Watch out for that one, the sergeant – he's a real bastard.'

The sergeant swung round from the far side of the room. 'Wat het jy gesê?' he snapped. That's the first time he hasn't paused, thought Arthur.

'I was just making a joke about his girl-friend's figure,' Koos replied easily, smiling at the girl as he said this. 'Shall I tell you too, Sergeant? No? All right. But won't you have a drop of brandy in your coffee?'

'Ek drink nie met kaffers nie.' The bastard, thought Arthur, the bloody racialist bastard. But Koos showed no reaction; he grinned at Arthur, shrugged his shoulders, and went out of the room again. Strange, thought Arthur, the only feelings I've had so far have been curiosity, rage, the usual lust, and a kind of cynicism – that's where all the attempted jokes come from. But no fear at all. Perhaps I'm like Koos – perhaps I've got so used to the idea of being searched by the police and being afraid that now it is actually happening I am not afraid, just as Koos can't get angry any more when he is insulted.

The sergeant had finished now – his last action was to look under the pillows of the bed and feel under the mattress; it was a cursory search, that last part. Perhaps he's realized that he's not going to find anything, Arthur thought. The pile on top of the desk was very small, one or two books and a pamphlet or newspaper; Arthur could not see what. The sergeant went to the doorway and called out to the other policemen, 'Are you two finished?' One was standing in the doorway of the bathroom; he came into the bedroom and said, 'Nothing there, Sergeant'. In a moment or two the third policeman came in, carrying a book, and followed by Henry. He must have come back while Koos was talking to me, thought Arthur; I wonder why he didn't say hullo.

'This is all I've found, Sergeant,' the policeman said, handing the book to the sergeant. It was a copy of Henry Miller's *Tropic of Capricorn.* Oh, the fool, the fool Henry, thought Arthur, I told him that it was banned and that he should get rid of it.

The sergeant looked at the book and then at Henry. 'Are you aware, Mr Naude, that this is a banned book?'

'I didn't know that it was in my room. Someone must have left it there and the maid stuck it in with my books.' Oh, you liar, thought Arthur, oh Henry, you beautiful liar.

The sergeant paused; again the non-stare. 'Possession of a banned book is an offence, Mr Naude.'

'I didn't possess it.'

'It was in your books, Mr Naude.' A pause again, then the

sergeant handed the book back to Henry. 'You'd better get rid of it, Mr Naude. You'd better get rid of it very soon.' That was lucky, thought Arthur.

The sergeant turned to Arthur. 'Now, Mr Devis, I want you to tell me what you are doing with these books,' and he pointed at the pile on the desk. Arthur went over to look at them. The pamphlet, he saw, was a report of the United Nations Special Committee on Apartheid. He picked it up and said, 'This is an official report, Sergeant; it's not banned. I had it solely because I am interested in international affairs.' He picked up one of the books – it was a novel, a very poor novel, he remembered, about the war against the French in Vietnam. The other was a novel too, an equally poor one, about the Dutch resistance against the Nazis. 'You are surely,' he said, 'not interested in or concerned with trash like this – why, I bought these to read on train journeys, at the station bookshop. They are nothing,' and he tossed them on to his bed.

The sergeant went over and picked up the books. Without looking at Arthur, he said, 'Tell me, Mr Devis, why are you so interested in civil wars?'

'Neither of these are about civil wars – they are novels, one about the Nazis, one about imperialists, imperialists like the British in the Transvaal in the Boer War.' As he said that, Arthur deliberately allowed his voice to rise, to give the impression of anger. 'Tell *me*, Sergeant van der Post, just what the hell is going on? You come in here, say that you're detaining me, search my room, bully my friends, and then accuse me of some unnamed crime for having two trashy novels and one serious pamphlet.'

'We are not accusing you of any crime, Mr Devis. We simply want to question you.'

'About what, Sergeant? About bad novels? Don't be a fool, Sergeant.'

Non-stare for fully fifteen seconds; then very quietly, 'No, you don't be a fool, Mr Devis. And don't call me a fool. It may interest you to know, Mr Devis, that we arrested a certain Mr Karl, or Charles, de Klerk in Johannesburg. We have good reason to suspect that you have a good deal of information about

Mr de Klerk and other people that may interest us. We have good reason to believe that you know a good deal about some objects which we found in the possession of Mr de Klerk.'

Arthur knew that his face and voice betrayed nothing as he turned away, replying, 'I don't know who or what you are talking about, Sergeant. I think it's a lot of nonsense.' But it isn't, he thought; it is bloody bad. This is no routine pick-up of a noisy university student; this is trouble. Why haven't the others tried to find me? Oh, God, they probably didn't know where I was tonight. Or perhaps they've been taken too. No, if the police have got Charlie, they'll probably start with me. I dare not try to warn them – Henry mustn't know anything at all. Christ, Charlie must have talked already, if they've come for me; has he given the lot?

The sergeant was talking to him. He hadn't heard. 'What did you say, Sergeant?'

'I said that you would make things much easier for yourself if you told us the whereabouts of the objects.'

'What "objects" are these?' Act, he told himself; act – look really puzzled.

'You know what objects, Mr Devis – things like what Mr de Klerk had. Where have you hidden them?'

'I haven't hidden anything, Sergeant. I don't know what you are talking about. I don't think you do either.'

'I know what I am talking about.' He emphasized the first 'I' and for the first time smiled. 'So do you. There is no urgency, Mr Devis; you will tell us what we want to know soon enough. Come. You will need a towel, soap, shaving-kit, toothbrush, clean clothes – and you better had bring a coat. We do not have central-heating in our cells.' So he's making the jokes now, thought Arthur.

When his bag was packed, he kissed the girl on the cheek, noticing as he did so that she had been crying, shook hands with Henry, telling him to look after the flat and to let his father know what had happened, and lastly shook hands with Koos, who grinned at him and winked encouragingly. Then the police and he left, one policeman walking in front carrying his bag, one walking next to him, and the sergeant walking behind. At the foot of the stairs Arthur stopped and looked up to the landing. Koos was leaning over the banister but he was not smiling any more. For the first time Arthur realized that he was very frightened.

Those were three of them; James Jeremy, whom nobody except his mother called anything but Jeremy, was taken at the same time as Arthur Devis by Sergeant Viljoen and three constables. While they were searching Jeremy's flat, Donald Quick arrived and was taken too. He had come only because he had not been able to get Jeremy's number, for Jeremy had taken it off the hook as he always did when he was in bed with Sheilagh; but the police let Sheilagh go, after she had stormed at them for trying to prevent her dressing alone in the bathroom. All the police did when she left was to put a car to tail her car and she led them straight to the garage where the major cache of equipment was – she was not meant to know about the cache but Jeremy had told her about that and about the organization; and she, loving him and believing in him, tried to help save him. Once they had the cache, the police arrested Sheilagh; and the first place they took her to was Jeremy's cell, so that they could taunt him and her.

Stevens was arrested two days later; and when he was arrested, the police met his protests without bothering to lie – 'Your friend Mr Jeremy has confessed, Mr Stevens; we know everything and you may as well start by telling the truth,' the Commandant told him, for by then the whole affair was in higher hands.

That is, in one way, nearly the whole story; but there is another way of telling it, a more difficult way, which takes a man where few need go. That is the way Quick went, though when he got there he hardly knew where he had been. Of the Johannesburg group, six escaped, two were taken; of the Port Elizabeth group, four escaped, two were taken; of the Grahamstown group, all three escaped. Of the national committee, Stevens and one other were taken, and one had been out of the country and didn't come back.

Jeremy said nothing, not when he opened the door to the police, not when the police found the papers, not when Quick arrived, not when Sheilagh left; only when he and Quick were handcuffed together before being taken out to the police-car did he say, 'They got the papers, Quick, they got the papers' – and Quick swore and said, 'Shut up, you bloody fool,' and Sergeant Viljoen, who heard, said nothing.

2

If you are lucky enough to make the drive from Johannesburg to Cape Town in mid-winter, and to be sixty miles from Cape Town on a clear night, when the moon happens to be shining, you may possibly see something that will make you feel what men must have felt when they first saw what they thought strange and beautiful and useless.

For, after the long reaches of the Highveld, the longer reaches of the Free State, and then yet again the long reaches of the Karoo, where the koppies and low ranges of hills seem nothing but a warning that somewhere in the world there may be something else other than the flat earth, it is, especially when they come as suddenly as they do at night, always almost incredible to reach the mountains of the Cape. But see them particularly on a mid-winter night, lightly disguised with snow and coloured by the sub-tropical moon, and you might think that you were descending into another world, a limbo of half-gods and half-men, where all judgement is suspended and where all that is left is to marvel.

Perhaps you feel that nothing matters except what is beautiful; but if you are not certain how important the beautiful is, this kind is easier to accept, because it can stand no compromise. It is so much the product of coincidence – mid-winter, clear night, moon shining, mountains, and snow in a country where the sun is always expected – that if you took away one element, the whole would be lost. You would be left with what is simply ordinarily beautiful, something most people could see, something which could be repeated anywhere, any time. But this coincidental beauty is so rare that (if you believe that anything exists outside your own mind and senses) you are bound to have it take on the force of a myth, say, the one night of a century when the old gods meet to celebrate, the one night when it is safe for them to leave their lairs to come walking the hills or, say, the night when the tribal chiefs met, each man alone, in such a place, to dispute for the control of a sub-continent. You may choose a particular myth and defend it; or you may choose to believe them all.

But go twenty miles further and already you will need a new myth. The moon will be higher, the bottom of the last pass before Cape Town reached, and before you will lie the thorn-dense, pondokkie-crowded, wind-naked Cape Flats; and, over above them, the afterthoughts of the escarpment, Table Mountain, Signal Hill, and Devil's Peak, and running away from them down towards Cape Point, the range they call Simonsberg. Over the flats to Cape Town, the sea all around, the Atlantic one side, the Indian the other, and in Cape Town, the people of both sides slung together, heaving. Still you need not judge, because Cape Town, say most South Africans, is easy-going, mediterranean (though the land lies between two oceans), less tortured, less modern, less industrial than Johannesburg; and if you close your eyes as you go past the townships, past Langa, past Nyanga, you may drive quietly into the comfortable suburbs and may even end your journey at that most beautiful of universities, in front of which Cecil John Rhodes dreams his dead dreams. So, goes the old Cape fable, above a city of old white houses and easy manners truth perches half-way up the mountain.

But now you may need a different myth, though you could stick to Adamastor sleeping noisily under Table Mountain. You could take the Flying Dutchman with its crew of ghosts and Van Hunks desiring to die at last, or you could take Woltemade, or Chief Makana, drowning as he tried to escape from Robben Island; for most people, what the Cape needs is a myth of heroes and traitors, not of sleepy gods nor even a myth of men of the sea meeting men of the land. So too you could be a modern man and try to make your myths from the people, from Sobukwe and Mandela and from Ernest Galo in his grave in Langa cemetery. But you still won't have it all, because neither one nor the other is true and because it is neither the one nor the other but is as much a bar full of drunken seamen in Salt River as it is naked girls in the sun at Clifton, as much the gables of Constantia as it is the corrugated iron of Nyanga, as much the sullen bus queues at five in the morning as the Presidential parades down Adderley Street.

Quick had done that journey many times before he met Jeremy; usually he didn't pick up hitch-hikers but this time, because it was in a dreary town called Edendale, because the hiker had on a university blazer, and because he was not just standing waving his thumb but was walking determinedly through the town, he did. This too was the first time that either of them had seen snow-covered mountains in the moonlight; and during the time that they were friends, and especially at times when it seemed that they would not be able to go on being friends much longer, they used to remind each other of that journey – they never actually talked about beauty but they both meant that, after dusk in the Karoo and through the night in the mountains, up to the time that Quick dropped Jeremy at the university, very early in the morning.

It seemed to both of them a good augury of their friendship that it started in so intense an experience. They did not say that, of course, because they were, in a way, a little ashamed of the intensity – they believed that human suffering mattered more than any natural beauty; they believed that the loveliness of the Cape was little more than an excuse for the beastliness of the townships; and they distrusted, as stupid or hypocritical, the people who loved Cape Town as the Tavern of the Seas, as the racial melting-pot, as liberal in instinct and gentle in demeanour. They talked about some of that during the journey; what neither saw was that the intensity of the experience depended on neither's having to share it fully, that what brought them together was a kind of mutual selfishness, each believing himself to be the centre of all judgement, the centre of all experience. If they had come through the mountains with a coach-load of friends, they would not have felt as deeply; this was a private experience – there happened to be two of them but neither really believed that the other felt quite as deeply as he did. They saw it together because they were forced to; just the two of them did, nobody else; and if each was prepared to take the other into his orbit, he was not prepared to acknowledge his dependence. That made them the half-gods, that made them heroes and traitors, that made them construct their own myths around their selves; but the centre had still to be the self.

Before Quick dropped Jeremy at the university, they had arranged to meet for lunch in two days' time. They were almost friends already; but each would say, even to himself, *Jeremy (or Quick) is my friend,* never *I am Jeremy's (or Quick's) friend.* They were friends but they did not share; it was almost because they could not share that they became friends.

From that time on they met regularly, sometimes alone, sometimes with girl-friends, sometimes with crowds of Jeremy's university friends; for Jeremy, though he could not be called popular at the university – he was too efficient, too ambitious – had a good many hangers-on, students who believed in the same things that he believed or who followed his fashion of thought, men and girls (boys called themselves men at eighteen, girls, who were often women by then, went on calling themselves girls) who were always ready for a political demonstration or to join a committee or to go to an integrated dance, and who would either abandon politics when they took their degrees or would go overseas, saying that they would be back but not really meaning it, and who would, in London or San Francisco, call themselves white Africans and would try to lose their South African accents as soon as they could. Quick didn't like many of them very much; he was himself a liberal but he was one by birth not conversion, and he was a pacifist as well, a pacifist who accepted revolution as inevitable, who almost believed in revolution, but who could not stomach what revolution meant. He could never, he said, join a political party except possibly one that he had himself founded and the policy of which he alone controlled. But if he didn't like many of the university liberals, he recognized that they were easier to be friends with than most of those he was thrown into contact with at his work, the journalists who wrote, he said, half-truths and whole lies for their families' sakes, the sub-editors who cursed censorship and who called Africans natives. Quick could afford to take a tough line on this – he had resigned his post on one newspaper on a matter of principle, whether the newspaper should appoint an African reporter to deal with township news. Quick wanted African reporters, he said, but he didn't want their reporting to be limited to local 'African' news only. But Quick hadn't suffered materially for his resignation since he had been offered a slightly better post on the rival Cape Town newspaper almost immediately.

So, gradually, Quick became part of Jeremy's university circle; he hadn't been to university himself, his family hadn't had enough money to put him through, and he hadn't been able to get a scholarship. But his home was full of books and he had always read widely; he was, in fact, much better read than any but the brightest of the students. When they discovered this as well as his advanced political views, they took him for their own; there was even some talk of raising a special scholarship for him to come to university but, when this didn't come to anything, they instead made sure that there was no party given to which he wasn't one of the first people invited or a decision taken where his advice on the publicity side not called for. Quick, for his part, enjoyed all this; he believed that he had missed a good deal in not going to university himself, he was only a few years older than most of them, and he enjoyed being listened to; and if sometimes he found them intolerably certain of themselves, he did too in a way enjoy that very certainty because he was then able to use his own uncertainties as ballast rather than sails.

But if Quick's acceptance into the university circle was at first gradual, the growth of the friendship between him and Jeremy was not – indeed, afterwards, Quick decided that the friendship had grown almost too fast, a greenhouse plant that died the moment someone let the night wind in. You can take your choice in South Africa – you can make your political friends your only friends and then be upset that, when the politics break up, your friendships lose their savour; or you can make friends and then try to involve your friends in your own politics. If a non-political friendship survives the politics, the politics may make it a special kind of friendship – when a man or woman has held fifteen years of imprisonment over your head and you still trust him or her completely, then you know that friendship is real. But you can't have friendship without politics; you can try but it doesn't work unless one side of the friendship loses, which is the same as changes, its politics. Their friendship started outside politics, or as far outside politics as Jeremy ever got; but their friendship grew in politics and, it if ever flowered at all, flowered in politics.

Quick, who believed that he could see his friends objectively, knew all the time that even in the politics there were things wrong with the friendship – he believed that Jeremy did not really understand history, or decline and fall. For Quick, the plateau was only interesting because of the cliffs that fell away from it; Jeremy, who called himself a realist in politics, was, Quick believed, really an optimist – he believed that the plateau, once reached, could be made a permanent home by either a benevolent dictator or democratic process. It didn't really matter very much because it was obvious to both of them that the plateau was still a very long way off; and even about the way of getting there there didn't need to be any argument. But the conflict was always there and it would, Quick decided later, always mean that they could never be as close to each other as each seemed to hope.

If that hampered the growth of their friendship permanently, what hampered its growth for only a short time was what Quick considered Jeremy's very annoying habit of secrecy, of seeming always to know something which he could not talk about, of half-beginning to tell Quick something that seemed very important before letting his revelation tail off into nonsense. Quick himself was thoroughly a journalist; he was temperamentally given to unbelief, the sort of man who makes jokes about the gods, half-seriously, and he was forced by his profession to be a sort of temporary sooth-sayer, revealing all for a moment – so he could not abide secrecy and if he enjoyed ambiguity it was for its usefulness rather than because he thought the truth was ambiguous. But after the first few months of his knowing Jeremy, he began to realize that Jeremy's secrecy was confined to especial areas; and he began to think that after all Jeremy knew things which he could not speak about, even to his close friends. At other times, he was convinced that the secretiveness was a pose to fulfil the need Jeremy had to seem more than he was.

Quick disliked particularly Jeremy's mysterious reference to his family; all Jeremy's friends knew that Jeremy had left home while he was still at school, that he had had a row with his mother which had ended with Jeremy's getting into her car and deliberately driving it at the side of the garage so hard that the car was a write-off, that he had persuaded his school not to accept his parents' cheque for his fees and had paid for his last year's schooling for himself out of money he made in the holidays, that his mother had got a Court Order that Jeremy was to return home, and that Jeremy's father had, for the one time in his life, stood up to his wife and had taken Jeremy's side before the Judge, who had then reversed his order. It was all part of Jeremy's glamour; and although he never talked of it himself, he always seemed to make it clear that his friends who accepted money from their parents were not entirely independent and that anyone who actually lived at home was a sell-out. Quick didn't mind that; though he loved his home, he had lived entirely independent of it ever since he had left school. What he did mind was that Jeremy was never open in what Quick thought was his hatred of his mother, that he never admitted that his father was a weakling, that he never spoke of his home. Quick, who seldom hesitated to say what he felt would aver love and hatred as easily as like or dislike – and loving his parents and being secure in their security, he could not understand that to hate your parents, or to love them not as a son usually loves his parents, meant too that you could not talk about them openly.

But gradually he began to think that Jeremy's secretiveness was because of something else too – he wasn't sure what it was, he wasn't sure that he would approve if he knew, but he knew that there was something else that Jeremy did have to cover up. At first he thought that it might be a love-affair, perhaps even a homosexual one; but he watched Jeremy closely and decided that it couldn't be that. What was it then? Was it only imagination? Was it only a pose? Was Jeremy involved in something illegal? Something political? Quick was used to building stories and theories from a basis of hints and guesses and he did so now; but before he had reached even the stage of constructing a story for himself Jeremy took him out of the range of guesswork.

It happened in the bar of the Mountain's Foot in the centre of

Cape Town. Quick always went in there for a drink between six and seven, before going back to his office for a final hour to check through his day's stories; and Jeremy had got into the habit of coming there, too, after his evening class in Economics at the town part of the University. So, because Jeremy and Quick tended to be there, others of their university friends often came in too. One evening, when Quick was sitting there having a drink with Mary Dobling, a post-graduate student whom he had begun to see regularly since his involvement in the university, they were both expecting Jeremy and he was a little late – Quick was just about to suggest that Mary come up to his office with him while he cleared his desk and then come to have dinner with him when Jeremy charged in, looking, as he often did, very busy, very worried.

'Hullo,' said Quick. 'Your class go on longer than usual?'

'No,' said Jeremy. 'I skipped it. Listen, Donald, have you seen Raymond Roseman in here?'

'No,' said Quick. He knew Roseman by sight only, knew that he was a liberal who worked for a large travel agency in Cape Town; but he had not been in – Quick always noticed when people who were not regulars went in and out of the bar-lounge; it was part of his skill as a journalist. 'Why? Were you expecting him?'

'I left a message that he was to join me here. He couldn't have got it.'

'Well, have a drink and wait for him.'

'I can't, I'm afraid – there's a bit of a rush on. Hell, I must see Roseman; it's vital.'

'Phone him at home,' said Mary.

'I've tried that.' Jeremy was curt. 'I can't get him anywhere. I wonder where the hell he is.'

Quick felt his impatience rise – this was what he hated about Jeremy, he thought; he'll say that things are urgent but he won't say what is urgent or why they are urgent. So he leaned back in his chair, looked at Jeremy still standing, his hand on the back of Mary's chair, and said, 'For goodness' sake, it can't be so urgent that you can't have one drink.'

Jeremy looked at his watch; he shook his head as if to say, We are not going to make it. Then he sat down. 'Look, I will have a drink – could you possibly get it while I write a note for Roseman?' he said.

Quick got up to go over to the bar while Jeremy took a notebook from his pocket and began to scribble in it; but no sooner had Quick come back with the beer that Jeremy always drank when Jeremy swore, tore the page out of the notebook, crumpled it up into a ball, and then put it and the notebook back into his pocket. 'It's no good,' he said. 'It won't work.'

'Is there anything that Mary and I can do?' said Quick. He was getting tired of what he thought was a performance for his and Mary's sake and hoped that his suggestion might stop Jeremy's pretence.

Jeremy leaned forward, looked at them quizzically, then said, 'All right. I know you both pretty well. Let's try it. Do you think that you could do something for me – something without asking any questions at all? There shouldn't be any risk involved and it isn't difficult.' Now Quick was interested; perhaps there was something going on. He was about to speak when Jeremy went on, 'I know it's a hell of a lot to ask but it really is important.'

Quick looked at Mary; she too was used to Jeremy's being secretive but now she looked interested – there might be something special here. He turned to look at Jeremy; 'Tell us what you want and we'll see if we can do it.'

'No,' said Jeremy. 'You must say that you'll do it before I tell you what it is I want you to do.'

'That's ludicrous, Jeremy. For God's sake, do you know what you've just said?'

Jeremy was almost frightening in his cold decisiveness. 'I know what I'm asking. Will you or won't you do it?'

Quick looked at Mary again – it was ludicrous, he knew, but he was too curious to refuse. Mary smiled at him, then nodded; so he turned to Jeremy to say, 'All right. We'll do it. Tell us what you want.'

'Thank you, man. It really is important. Have you got your car here?'

'No, but Mary has hers.'

'All right. Finish your drinks and let's go.'

'May I call in at my office on the way?' said Quick; he acted as if he were plaintive. It was a way of showing that he was choosing to let Jeremy bully him.

Jeremy looked at his watch again. 'We haven't really got time,' he said. 'Can't you leave it until tomorrow?'

'I suppose so,' said Quick. 'There's nothing really urgent.'

In Mary's car Jeremy explained what he wanted them to do – they were to drive over to the airport, leave their car in the car-park, wait until 8.15 exactly, go into the terminal building, walk up to a man who would be standing just to the right of the restaurant doors with a small but heavy parcel, wrapped in blue paper, under his right arm, greet him as if they knew him, all go into the airport bar for a drink, and then they were to leave soon afterwards, taking the parcel with them and leaving the man behind in the bar. They were then to deliver the parcel straight to Jeremy at his flat. That was all.

Quick wanted to know, first, why Jeremy was not coming with them. 'I can't explain why, Donald. I'm sorry but I can't. I just can't come with you,' Jeremy said. Then Quick wanted to know what would happen if they by any chance got the wrong man. Jeremy's answer was impatient: 'Look, man, the coincidence is improbable; anyway, if you go up to someone and greet him as if you know him, and then he doesn't seem to know who you are, you'll know that you've got the wrong man. But there won't be many parcels wrapped in blue paper. Don't worry, Donald, there's nothing to it.'

Quick was not particularly convinced; but Mary shushed him and told Jeremy that they would do it exactly as he had asked. So they dropped Jeremy at his flat and went on to the airport, without any trouble; by 9.30 they had delivered the parcel back to him.

Mary seemed content to know nothing more; but Quick was not. He realized that Jeremy would probably not talk in front of Mary; so he waited until it was late and she said that she had to go back to her university residence, so he refused her offer of a lift and said that he would go home by bus, so he ignored her disappointment and let her go alone. Then he began to tax Jeremy with questions; he asked but could not get one definite reply; Jeremy would not even tell him what was in the parcel and Quick, though he had several ideas of what it might be, did not have the courage to ask him outright what it was.

In the end, Jeremy, realizing how much Quick needed to know, said, 'Listen, if I could tell you I would; but I can't. It's not in my hands to decide that you should know; I asked you to fetch this parcel only because it was essential that someone fetch it and it couldn't be me.'

'Was Roseman meant to fetch it? Was that why you wanted him?'

'That's pretty obvious, isn't it? Roseman was meant to arrange for it to be fetched but the time had to be changed. I can't, really I can't, tell you anything more.'

'So Roseman is involved in what you're doing?'

'Look, Donald, don't ask any more questions. I'd tell you if I could; but I can't. As it is, I'm beginning to think that I shouldn't have asked you.'

Quick was deeply hurt by this last remark; up to that time he had thought that Jeremy was really enjoying being secretive, that he was concealing whatever he knew so that Quick would have to worm it out of him. Now he knew that, if it was bad enough that Jeremy should not trust him with knowledge of what was going on, it was even worse that Jeremy should be beginning to doubt the wisdom of having asked for his help at all. So he stopped asking questions and said only, 'Well, if you can't tell me, you can't. But you needn't think that I'll mention to anyone that I fetched the parcel.'

'I didn't think that you would, Donald. If I had I wouldn't have asked you,' and Jeremy smiled that sudden gentle, charming smile that confused so many people into thinking that he was really gentle and really charming. Quick knew that he wasn't, knew that he was very tough and very cold, and loved him for those qualities as much as he enjoyed the calculated charm.

There was not an end to the secrecy; but Quick knew now that there was something to be secretive about and that made it easier for him to bear. He still longed for Jeremy to speak openly about his family; but it was a longing that he got used to – it did not slow the friendship down, in some ways it speeded it up, since

Quick would listen so carefully to all Jeremy said, listen for hints, listen for ambiguities, listen for the unexpected revelation of feeling. So night after night they would talk half-way through the night, about politics, about race, about history, about poetry, about journalism, about philosophy, and everything except what Quick didn't yet know was the organization, about everyone except Jeremy's mother and father. Their friends began to accept that these two were close; and Mary Dobling and Sheilagh Owen became friends too, because it seemed a good way to keep close to the person they wanted.

3

In the early days, after Ian Stevens had put to Raymond Roseman and James Jeremy the basic idea of sabotage of governmental and industrial installations without violence to people, and before anyone else was recruited to the Cape Town group, they believed that the future of the organization was as a primarily African one, working with the African nationalists, working under the orders of the African nationalist organizations if necessary. So Jeremy, it was decided, should try to get in touch with the leaders of the nationalist movements in the Cape area; but even then it was not easy, for the nationalist organizations had been declared illegal and there had been enough people gaoled for everyone to be cautious. Still, Jeremy managed it well, as he managed most things of that kind; he talked to the few African students still at the University, very generally at first, until he singled out the man they seemed to regard as their spokesman – it happened to be someone whom Jeremy knew well, a man called Jameson or Moshi Ndoli (Jameson was his 'English' name, Moshi his 'African' name – so Jeremy called him Moshi while most other students called him Jameson). Most of the African students at the University kept themselves very much to themselves, for they were tolerated rather than accepted there; but Jeremy they were prepared to trust, for he was outspoken, violent, one of the new breed of radical students who were almost ashamed to call themselves liberals and who used that title only to distinguish themselves from the communists, of whom there were not very many, anyway. So Jeremy took the risk and spoke openly about what he wanted to Ndoli, and Ndoli was persuaded, and, after a fortnight, arranged a meeting in one of the townships between Jeremy and Roseman and three representatives of the Africanist Congress. Stevens, it had been agreed, would not get involved at that stage; if anything went wrong he would be able to try again.

Ndoli came to Roseman's house in Sea Point to guide them to the meeting. 'You will not be able to enter the township through the usual route,' he said, 'so I will take you round the railway line at the back and then cross the lines, go into the township through the cemetery and then to the right house.' Roseman did not like Ndoli much; he was, it seemed, a loudmouth, likely to say that white liberals were foolish and insincere, but not likely to help them be more sincere. Jeremy, however, was prepared to forgive him almost everything, now that he had got the meeting set up; and now, taking a hand off the steering wheel of Roseman's car, he signalled under cover of the front seat that Roseman should not worry – first a movement of his hand to show doubt, then thumbs up.

Whatever Roseman's doubts, the meeting was properly organized – and Ndoli was one of the three representatives there. Jeremy, though he was surprised when he realized how important Ndoli was, smiled at Roseman when he saw this, as much as to say, He's all right, you see – but though Jeremy himself could relax, Roseman could not. He found himself a seat in the corner and left most of the talking to Jeremy, while he watched the faces of the Africans. One of them Roseman had seen before at various protest meetings in the city, a small sombre man, with a badly deformed lower lip – one of the results of two years in Leeukop prison, so it was said – and dressed in the dark blue overalls of any working man. The lip made it difficult to hear what he said; he seemed to spit his words rather than speak them. The other man, whom neither of them knew by sight, was more impressive to look at, a big man, very black, dressed like a business man or a headmaster. Ndoli waited until they were all sitting, then introduced them, the white men first. The man with the deformed lip was Seboko – when he heard the name, Roseman smiled at him and nodded; he remembered now that they had been introduced, two years before, at some Embassy party. These days neither he nor Seboko were invited to those kind of parties. The other man was Madube; Jeremy could not help himself and whistled when he heard that name – most people at all involved in politics had heard of Madube though few knew why they had heard of him; he was reputed to be one of the protégés of the Chief, though his politics had outstripped the Chief's years before. Nobody was sure exactly what he did or what position he held but it was sometimes rumoured that he spent almost as much time outside South Africa as in, crossing the borders illegally to visit the Heads of African States and then doing what few people risked doing, coming back into the country. At any rate, both Jeremy and Roseman knew that if Moses Madube was at the meeting, it meant that it was being seriously treated.

The conversation was, at first, very general – Roseman was pleased by this because it gave him time to adjust to the situation; he could not help it but he felt a little ridiculous coming to such a meeting with men whom he thought would not have all that much interest in their ideas. All the same, when Seboko asked him if he went to Embassy parties still, he was glad to be able to reply that he did not get invited any more and to be able to joke about it with Seboko; it made him feel much easier to share at least that. Jeremy, on the other hand, was impatient; he wanted to talk hard, he wanted to convince Madube that he was in earnest, he wanted to talk about plastic explosives, railway lines, fuses, pylons, training a cell-system; as the conversation meandered along he got more and more restless and even tried to force the meeting to the point. But Seboko wasn't having any; he did much of the talking and he kept it very general – Moses Madube didn't speak at all, he grunted once or twice in what Roseman and Jeremy hoped was assent, but true to his first name he was not a spokesman.

After what seemed to Jeremy a long time of pointless chatter, a woman came into the room carrying a tray of tea things. Everyone in the room except Madube stayed sitting when she came in, though Jeremy, when he saw Madube get up, did so too. Madube greeted her with great formality, took the tray, made her sit in his chair, refused Jeremy's chair, poured out the tea, handed it around, starting with the woman, and then, when everyone had a cup of tea and a biscuit, sat down on the edge of the table and said, 'Now shall we talk business, gentlemen?'

Jeremy was uneasy now; he had not expected a woman to be

present and no attempt had been made to introduce her; he must have showed what he felt, for Madube spoke again, 'Oh, I am sorry, gentlemen, I forgot that you would not know my wife; Mrs Madube, Mr Jeremy and Mr Roseman. I hope that you will not mind her being present – Mr Seboko and Mr Ndoli won't, I know, but I have asked her in to the meeting because she is a better judge of sincerity than I am.' Now Jeremy was angry; he looked at Roseman and saw that he too had reacted badly to Madube's last remark. It was made worse for both of them by the fact that Ndoli was obviously enjoying their discomfort. Damn it, thought Jeremy, if we weren't so bloody wet we'd walk out right now, telling Madube that he can get stuffed; but we can't afford to do that.

But Seboko, sensing their anger, spoke now; 'I am sure,' he hissed, 'that Mr Madube does not mean to impute that you are insincere' – he spoke English as if he had never used it except in a meeting or from a platform – 'You will understand that we are risking a great deal in meeting you here.'

Jeremy, who had been ready to forgive Madube for his remark, flared up at the last: 'We are risking a good deal in coming here ourselves,' he snapped at Seboko.

'True,' said Seboko, 'but, Mr Jeremy, we are risking a whole organization, a mass organization. You, I take it, are here representing no one really but yourselves.'

'We have other people interested,' said Jeremy.

'But it is a few, not many. I do not intend blame on you for this – sadly, it is in the nature of things. Otherwise we would not have to meet here.' Seboko paused; neither Jeremy nor Roseman could say anything. 'But could you,' he went on, 'tell us now exactly in what you are interested?'

'I thought Moshi had told you when he arranged the meeting,' said Jeremy.

'Moshi?' said Seboko; he did not seem to recognize the name.

'Yes, Moshi,' Jeremy repeated. 'You know, Moshi . . .' he said the name very distinctly but because Seboko didn't seem to know what he meant he said, 'Moshi Ndoli.'

'You mean Jameson?' said Madube.

'Yes,' said Jeremy. He looked at Ndoli. He was looking at the floor, very embarrassed.

'I see,' said Madube, grinning at his wife and at Seboko. 'I see. Moshi is the name you use at the university instead of Jameson, is it, Mr Ndoli?'

Ndoli nodded, not saying anything; got you, thought Jeremy – a fair return for laughing at us before.

'Moshi is a good name,' said Madube, 'but then so is Jameson.' He allowed himself to savour the joke for a few moments more, then let the smile die from his face, and said, 'But we have no time for names now. Will you go on, please, Mr Seboko?'

Seboko had allowed himself to smile for only a moment or two; now he said, 'Mr Ndoli did tell us what you told him, Mr Jeremy. But we want to hear it again from you, in your voice,' he paused, 'not of course because we think that Mr Ndoli did not get it completely right.' Jeremy realized that Seboko was making sure that Ndoli was not upset at the joke Madube had made; he looked at Ndoli but could not see if he was embarrassed only or embarrassed and angry. Then he looked at Roseman, who signed that he was content that Jeremy should speak for both of them; so very quickly and very quietly, he outlined their plans. He spoke so quietly that everyone had to lean forward to hear what he said; and his exposition was so masterly that Roseman, who had heard it often before and knew the arguments by heart, found himself leaning forward so that he would miss nothing.

When he had finished, the four Africans didn't say anything for several minutes; you could see that they were searching the argument for loopholes and limitations. Then Madube said something in Xhosa to Seboko, who began to question Jeremy closely about the details of their plans – gradually it became clear that what he really wanted to know was nothing to do with intention or principle but simply the practical details; where would they get explosives, where would they store them, what kind of objects they would aim at? These, of course, were the questions that Jeremy and Roseman found it most difficult to answer, for, although they had worked out the organization in principle and had a plan of action, they knew little yet of the details of sabotage. On the one hand they realized that Seboko himself knew almost nothing about the actual process of sabotaging something, but on the other they could sense that he was losing interest as their answers became necessarily more and more tentative; and because they tried harder and harder to be specific, they became more and more vague as they searched among detail for points they could answer firmly. They were just beginning to despair when Ndoli spoke from his corner – 'Can you get guns?' he said.

'What?' said Jeremy, though he had heard perfectly well. He looked at Roseman.

'Can you get guns?' repeated Ndoli. Jeremy looked at Madube and Seboko; but neither of them seemed very surprised at the question. 'You don't seem to understand,' Jeremy began, 'that our organization is aimed at objects rather. . . .' But Mrs Madube interrupted him, speaking for the first time now; she spoke not in English but in Xhosa; and she seemed angry, particularly with Ndoli – she had a very light voice for such a large woman but it carried force; all three men listened to her attentively. She must be able to understand English, thought Jeremy; I wonder if she ever speaks it.

When she had finished speaking, Mr Madube spoke to the others in Xhosa too. Whatever she had said, the three African men seemed to have accepted it. Ndoli said no more about guns and Seboko said several complimentary things, how they were happy to find white liberals prepared to demonstrate their beliefs to the extent of committing sabotage and so on; but with the doubt introduced by Ndoli's question to work on their minds, the two white men began to realize that Seboko was not going to commit himself to any definite agreement to co-operate though he did not rule co-operation out.

Roseman, though not Jeremy, had been prepared for this reaction and was about to try to explain why, although they were unable to give exact details, a promise of co-operation, if it was only a promise that there should be another meeting in a few months' time, was so necessary to them, when there was a soft knock at the front door. Seboko was on his feet and out of the room, taking his empty cup and saucer with him, almost before the knocking was finished. Mrs Madube went to the door, opened it, and let in a small African boy. He gabbled something in Xhosa to her and, without waiting for a reply, ran back down the path to the open garden gate. Mrs Madube turned to speak to her husband, Ndoli went forward to join them, the three spoke, and then Ndoli turned to Jeremy and Roseman to say, 'The small boy says that the police are on their way here; I must take you away.' Madube added, very quietly, 'Someone must have seen you come here; it is strange that nothing has happened before but that boy is the son of a policeman.' Then he and Mrs Madube shook hands with both of the white men very formally and, they realized, very warmly. Ndoli took Roseman by the arm and directed him towards the kitchen, Jeremy following. As he was crossing the room Mrs Madube said something in Xhosa to her husband, and Jeremy, thinking that she was going to say something to him, stopped and half-turned; but when he heard that it was Xhosa, he started for the door again, only to be stopped by Mr Madube's soft voice. 'Mr Jeremy,' he said, my wife asks me to tell you that she thinks that you are a very brave young man and that she blesses you for your courage.' Jeremy turned, about to try to say thank you to both of them, but Ndoli didn't give him time, came back, took him by the arm, and led him out of the kitchen door to where Roseman was waiting.

From the Madube's house they walked quickly, keeping to the shadows and to dark lanes, back to and through the cemetery, to the railway line, where they left Ndoli. Roseman went straight up the bank and over the lines to the car, saying only 'Good-bye' to Ndoli. But Jeremy stopped for a moment, shook hands, and said, 'Good-bye; and thank you, Moshi.' He emphasized the name, Moshi, trying to show that he understood why Ndoli did not want the name Jameson; he could not see Ndoli's face in the darkness. Then he turned and began to climb the railway embankment. At the top he stopped and looked down; he could just see Ndoli in the darkness below the bank. As Jeremy looked, he took a half-pace forward, almost as if he were going to follow them; but he came no further forward and, it seemed to Jeremy, waved at him to go away. For a moment, Jeremy understood what must be in Ndoli's mind; he and Roseman were going back to their white lives in the white suburbs – for a moment, it must have seemed almost like freedom. As Jeremy watched, Ndoli turned, climbed through the fence, and started back through the cemetery towards the township; and then Roseman revved the engine of the car and Jeremy turned and ran over the lines and down the other side of the embankment.

Mr Madube was arrested that night and Seboko and Ndoli soon afterwards. But there seemed to be no connection made between the Africans and Roseman, Jeremy and Stevens. For a time they thought that they might go too; but when, three weeks later, Madube, Seboko, Ndoli, and fourteen others were charged with belonging to an unlawful organization, they realized that whoever had given the information had either not known about the meeting or had not given enough for the police to pick them up too. Near the end of the trial, Jeremy actually went into the court and sat with the other spectators from the university. After all, he explained to himself, it was no risk to their organization, since Ndoli was known to be one of his associates at the university. Madube got twelve years, Seboko, ten, and Ndoli five; the sentences of the other fourteen ranged from seven years to six months. After Ndoli had been sentenced, he turned to wave at the students in the back of the court; and it seemed to Jeremy that Ndoli searched his face out before he waved again, the same go-away sign that he used at the railway line near the cemetery. Jeremy knew then that neither Ndoli nor the others had said a word about their meeting; and when, leaving the court, he walked past Mrs Madube and she pretended not to recognize him, he knew that they could go on with their work. From that time on, however, they had no illusions that they would be able to work with other organizations. They were entirely on their own.

Their first task, they knew, was to recruit more members to the Cape Town group; it was, they knew too, perhaps the most dangerous part of their work. Even then people were getting used to the idea that every next man might be an informer; and they could not go to the obvious choices, because the people who were obviously likely to be willing to join them would be obvious to the Security police too. So they began to search for recruits. They would not need many, they knew; three for the time being and probably for ever, since you couldn't, said Stevens, expect the group, let alone the organization, to survive for more than two years. Roseman and Jeremy knew that there were other groups being started in the other provincial centres; but they were told nothing about them, nor did Stevens seem to know anything. He kept telling them that he had been approached by someone else, someone whom he wouldn't name but who, he let them understand, knew all about the organization nationally. That someone had suggested that he approach Roseman and Jeremy; but theirs were the only names he had had. He hadn't even any more suggestions; after all, he knew so few people.

Roseman and Jeremy, who knew little about Stevens except that he was virtually a recluse and that he was supposed to be the person who financed several more or less left-wing publications and organizations, were forced to agree that he could do no more recruitment. So they agreed that Roseman should make some suggestions – he was not, they agreed, to approach anyone himself, he was simply to suggest suitable names to Stevens and Jeremy.

After two weeks he produced a list of five names, three of which he had himself marked with queries. Stevens and Jeremy rejected the other two almost immediately and, when Stevens asked Roseman whether he could suggest more names, Roseman admitted that he probably couldn't. 'Everyone I think of,' he said, 'is either too well-known to be much use or else isn't free of our suspicions, even if they are pretty tenuous ones.' So Stevens turned to Jeremy and asked if he could find anyone; Jeremy, who had already thought of several people, said that he would try but that he would need at least a month for his inquiries – he did not want, though he did not say this, to make the same mistake that Roseman had made.

It was now that what amounted to Jeremy's genius for organization showed. First he made a list of possible recruits. He cut his list in half simply by taking off the names of those who were married, those who lived with parents or relations, or those who seemed likely to marry the girls they took out. This left ten names. He then took from the list the names of the four people who might too easily be supposed to be his closest friends. About the six left on the list he made as many inquiries as he safely could, never asking anyone directly what he thought of So-and-so, but still finding out where they came from, who their friends were, where they worked or how they paid their university fees, what their opinions were, and how tough they seemed; he went to parties, talked to them in groups, noisily, talked to them in quiet corners; he looked at what motor-cars they drove and if they drove; he calculated how much their clothes cost; and in doing so he cut his list down to three. Of each of these he felt sure; so he double-checked his findings and decided that he was not sure of one of them. This left two.

He was meant to go back to Stevens and Roseman with his two names but he did not for, having got that far, he decided to recruit both without consulting anyone else; after all, he thought, it was very unlikely that either Stevens or Roseman would be able to add anything to what he had discovered. The first was a man called Hunter – a university student, though older than most, thirty-five or thirty-six, a Britisher not a South African, who had done national service with the British Army in Malaya, who had then taken a commission and had stayed on in the Army for another five years, serving mainly in the Near East, before resigning his commission to go farming in Southern Rhodesia. His farm had been a failure and, after two or three years, he had sold it and gone to the University of Cape Town, where he was reading for a degree in Social Anthropology. He worked hard, spent every day in the library and, on the basis of the results of his first two years, was commonly expected to get a first-class degree. He did not seem to have many friends and those he had were mainly not whites, a Coloured student, a few Indian teachers, and an African lecturer whose best student he was. He didn't, as far as Jeremy could work out, have a steady girl and although he seemed to have enough money to manage comfortably, he was obviously not rich; he seemed to live fairly comfortably but he drove a very beat-up Landrover.

One afternoon, when most of the students had gone home or back to their university residences, and at a time when those few who stayed to work in the library would be either engrossed in their books or asleep over them, Jeremy went into the library and up to the Anthropology Division where he knew Hunter would be working. He sat down next to Hunter, took from his inside pocket a single type-written sheet, which he unfolded and laid in front of Hunter. Hunter read it through twice, then folded it again and gave it back to Jeremy. Jeremy stood up and walked out of the library; Hunter would, he was certain, follow him. Once they were outside, Jeremy stopped and said to Hunter, 'Are you interested?'

'Yes,' said Hunter, 'I've been wondering what you were up to.'

'You mean, checking up on you?'

'Watching me,' said Hunter.

'I hadn't realized you'd noticed.' Hunter did not say anything so Jeremy went on, 'I hope it didn't offend you.'

'No,' said Hunter, 'though I was getting suspicious.'

'But you are interested in what the document said.'

'Yes,' said Hunter. 'I've been hoping for something like this for two years or more now. I was beginning to think that everyone was asleep. But I'll want to know a great deal more.'

'Of course,' said Jeremy, but Hunter did not let him finish what he intended to say.

'I realize that you won't be able to tell me that without something firm from me. So let me tell you something that you couldn't have found out. I had a special job in the army – while I was doing my service in Malaya. . . .'

'I know that,' said Jeremy.

'Of course,' said Hunter. 'But let me finish. While I was doing service, I was trained particularly to dismantle booby traps – and that meant, of course, any kind of sabotage weapon.'

'And no one else knows this? Here, I mean?' asked Jeremy.

'There's just a chance that your Security police have it, if their links with Britain are close. But I don't think so. I wasn't very high in the Army ever; and I've never had any trouble about security coming here from Rhodesia.'

Jeremy's excitement at Hunter's news was beginning to show, for Hunter smiled and said, 'I've kept very quiet about that. I hoped it might be useful one day. Are you prepared to take me on now?'

'We won't want you for dismantling things,' Jeremy joked.

'I know,' said Hunter, 'not in the usual sense of the word anyway.'

'And there's no money in it,' said Jeremy; that had to be said, he knew, sooner or later – it was his only worry about Hunter.

'I'm not a mercenary, if that's what you are asking me.' Hunter stopped and turned away; he seemed to be looking for the right words; then he went on, 'You know, this may sound strange coming from an ex-Army officer, an expert in explosives, an ex-farmer from Rhodesia, but I hate and loathe what is happening in this country so much that I can scarcely speak of it. I'd do almost anything if I thought it might help to change things here, and that's even if change meant chaos for a good long time.'

'I know,' said Jeremy. 'I know and I live here,' and he and Hunter walked down towards the line of trees that hemmed the University off from the State forestry lands.

Jeremy's next recruit was, on the surface, a more peculiar choice; he was a young student called Arthur Devis, a medical student in his third year who, after only narrowly passing his first two yearly exams, seemed now to be trying to cut his third as fine, for he spent more time drinking and womanizing than he ever thought of working, driving too fast in a white sports car from a rugby match to a bar to a party to his latest girl's house, where her father would come downstairs from his bed to protest at the noise and would, more likely than not, end by opening a new bottle of brandy for his daughter's boyfriend and drinking a good deal of it himself. Arthur had, it was agreed by all his teachers and a good many of his friends, always had too much money; his father was a director of companies and Arthur himself had inherited, before he was ten, a fortune from his grandfather.

Almost any of these things would have made Jeremy despise Arthur Devis; but, a year before, Jeremy had been invited to a debate in the Medical School, to propose the motion 'That Liberal Humanism is Outmoded'. There had been only a handful of people there; and Jeremy had not said very much of what was in his mind, preferring to save it for some more important occasion;

he had simply tried to argue that what South Africa needed was something much tougher than liberalism. His opponent had been a well-meaning fifth-year medical student who, Jeremy decided, had obviously not understood one word in the whole of Jeremy's speech; and it seemed that the debate was about to peter out into nothingness when Devis, sitting right at the back, jumped up and began to attack all South African liberals including Jeremy. At first Jeremy thought, Oh it's just the same old hackneyed stuff, and he began to prepare some phrases for his summing-up that would show clearly that his own attitude was to the left, not the right, of South African liberals; that would at least take the wind out of the clichés. But suddenly Devis began to talk what Jeremy thought was sense. He said, 'I am not a nationalist. I am not a fascist. I am not a liberal and I am not a communist. I suppose I'm too rich to be a communist. But I do think that this country's going to all hell, that it has been going there for three hundred years, that no amount of liberal talk is going to stop that and that anything less than liberalism is going to get us to hell quicker. And now I am going to have a bloody big drink,' and he started noisily to leave the meeting. Jeremy shouted out above the laughter of the audience, 'Eh, wait for me,' said sorry to the chairman, and left as his opponent stood up to mumble something about respecting his opponent's views. Jeremy caught Devis before he got to the entrance of the building.

That night they had talked for two hours in a bar and, after Devis had driven him home, for three hours in Jeremy's flat. As the evening went on, Jeremy who, perhaps because he was himself so secretive, never found it difficult to make other people talk about themselves, realized that all Devis's flamboyance covered not the emptiness of too much money and too little thought but the emptiness of despair. He realized that before he discovered the cause; but the cause made him understand where the speech had suddenly burst from, where all the despair came from. Devis, Jeremy discovered, had had, while he was still at school, a love affair with a Coloured girl a little older than himself; he had met her, he said, at a jazz club he used to go to. Somebody, one of the girl's friends perhaps, had informed on them to the police, the police had arrested them and had charged them for contravening the Immorality Act. Devis's father, when he found out, had bribed the police not to press the charges; it had cost him a good deal, for the police had already entered the charges and that meant that not only the two policemen who had made the arrests but the desk sergeant and the secretary who entered the charges had to be paid. With the charges removed, Arthur's father had offered the girl two hundred pounds and a job in Durban, if she would agree not to see his son again. She had, 'naturally', said Arthur, accepted; his bitterness was not for the girl's accepting but for his father's tempting. He would, he said to Jeremy, rather have been charged than see that happen; and where before, he said, his father had been almost like his brother, he had seemed suddenly like a policeman, a clever policeman.

Jeremy and Devis had not really become friends, even after that night; their interests lay too far apart and Devis needed his hectic life as much as Jeremy needed his intense one. But they would meet, more often than anyone realized, usually when Devis needed to talk to someone from whom he did not have to conceal what he felt. It seemed even that Devis was beginning to settle down; he passed, though again only narrowly, the exams at the end of his third year; he began to share a flat with Henry Naude and, although he still drank a good deal and seemed not to stay with any one girl for longer than two nights, he would often appear at political meetings at the university and would sometimes even speak. It would be, his disappointed friends said, almost a reformation if it weren't for the politics.

So now, when Jeremy had decided that Devis would do, he went to find him and told him straight what he wanted him for. Devis agreed at once, as Jeremy had known he would; but it was not simply that the almost quiet life was beginning to pall for Arthur, it was also that, once he had given his allegiance to someone, he would not take it back until the last possible moment.

Jeremy went back to Roseman and Stevens with these two; though he was half-expecting trouble for having recruited them without the group's permission. Stevens seemed to accept his action as if he had expected it – Roseman was less happy, obviously, but it was difficult for him to be more than superficially annoyed when Jeremy had found someone like Hunter for the group. Soon it became apparent that Devis too would be useful, for it was he who, on a special visit to the Transvaal, found Charlie de Klerk and who bribed him to steal explosives from the factory at which he was overseer and who, by drink and charm and money, kept a supply of explosives coming from de Klerk to all the groups.

With those five, the Cape Town group needed only one more person to be complete, although it could and did function with only five – that sixth person, whom Hunter had to be persuaded was not a luxury addition, had to be someone with an almost impeccable cover, someone who could move around the Cape easily without being thought to travel too much or too quickly, preferably someone who had reason for visiting the areas which the group had selected, both before and after the operations though after was more important. Jeremy knew, before Stevens had finished his outline of the functions that a sixth member could fulfil, that the obvious person was Quick – but he did not really want Quick, he thought; he wasn't sure why but he didn't want him, simply because he was a friend, perhaps. In fact, it was Devis who suggested Quick; he had met him one night in Jeremy's flat and now he said, 'What about your mate Donald Quick, Jeremy? He's a journalist, isn't he? He'd be able to visit the scene of the crime and no questions asked.'

'I don't think Donald would do,' said Jeremy. 'He's a pacifist, for one thing.'

'What better cover than that?' laughed Devis. 'The pacific saboteur, eh?'

'I think he really believes in it,' said Jeremy, carefully.

'If I understand correctly, Mr Stevens,' said Hunter, 'this member wouldn't have to do anything with the actual material, would he?'

'He might have to help with transport,' said Roseman.

'If Quick would join us, I don't think that would really worry him, provided that he wasn't expected to do anything more than that,' said Jeremy. Up to that moment he had forgotten about the parcel that Quick had fetched from the airport; he wanted to know more then, thought Jeremy – if he found out, would he come in properly?

'He's hardly a pacifist, then, is he?' said Roseman.

'I suppose that we could put him up to it on the basis of our distinction between violence to objects and violence to people,' said Jeremy.

'You mean,' went on Hunter, 'the distinction drawn as a matter of principle and not simply as what was convenient?'

Roseman could not allow this; 'Some of us,' he said, 'believe this as a matter of principle already. . . .' But Stevens realized that he could not allow this discussion to develop; it might, he knew, be interesting – the part of him that was intellectual longed to have the argument out, once and for all, but the part of him that was politician knew that it was a rock on which the group could flounder. It had to be stopped and so he said, simply, 'I think that what Quick believes isn't really what we are discussing – we are talking about whether he would be good as the sixth member. What he believes is really Jeremy's problem; since Jeremy would do the actual recruiting and would, presumably, have to find out if he'd accept before he asked him in.'

'Hear, hear,' said Hunter; Stevens looked at him in surprise – he had thought that Hunter had been trying to provoke an argument. Then Hunter went on; 'This Quick is considered a fairly well-known journalist, is he?' He was asking Jeremy.

'I think he's supposed to be pretty good.'

'I mean,' said Hunter, 'he would be able to choose to write a story on railway sabotage if he wanted to, once we got going – he would get the police's co-operation in collecting information.'

'I'm not sure about the police,' said Jeremy. 'Donald tends to argue an awful lot with them, about things like regulations about going into the townships.'

'But he'd still be able to cover the events? He'd still get news from his colleagues? For example, he'd be quite likely to get advance news that the police were tightening up in some area, wouldn't he?' Hunter pressed.

'As much as anyone outside the police would,' Jeremy said.

'He sounds the right man, doesn't he?' said Hunter. 'What do you think, Mr Stevens?'

Stevens avoided the question by asking, 'What do you think, Arthur?'

'I suggested him in the first place,' said Devis, 'and if Jeremy is happy then so am I.'

'And you, Roseman?'

'I'd like to know why Jeremy didn't suggest him himself.'

Jeremy smiled. 'I suppose simply because he's a very close friend of mine. We don't really want this as a society of close friends, do we?'

'No,' said Hunter; and so Stevens went on, 'But Quick does sound as if he might suit the job. Will you approach him yourself, Jeremy?'

'I'd rather not, if you don't mind. I'd rather you did, Ian. Couldn't I bring him here to meet you? Roseman could come too, of course.'

'I don't think there'd be any need of that, do you, Ian?' said Roseman. 'I'm prepared to leave it to you.'

'So that's all right, is it? Good,' said Stevens. 'There are just two other things. First, we shan't be able to use this place again for meetings. You've been here three or four times already and that is too often. If Quick comes in I'd suggest that he be asked to organize any meetings that we have to have; though I hope that once we get going there won't have to be many. Also, I don't want anyone to phone me from now on except in emergencies. Is that agreed?' The four other members of the group nodded. 'The other thing is that Hunter has something to say.'

'Not really to say,' said Hunter. 'But I have here five envelopes each containing five sheets of paper; on the sheets are abbreviated instructions about the handling of explosives and various simple methods of laying them. The best thing that you can do is to learn these by heart and then destroy them; but they are very complicated so you may have to keep them,' and he handed one to each man, keeping one back for himself.

'As a matter of interest,' said Roseman, 'why are you keeping one for yourself? You must know it and more by heart already.'

'So that you will know that I have accepted the same instructions,' Hunter replied. Then he smiled and said, 'And they are strict, you see – I don't want you trying experiments and I don't expect that you would want me to do clever things that you could not control if anything went wrong with me. So I need the instructions, too.'

Devis, who had opened his envelope to look at the sheets, could not hold back his question, 'But why aren't they in code? I mean, anyone could understand these.'

Hunter's reply was in the voice of the practised officer; 'Codes,' he said, 'codes mean nothing. If something is in code, you tend to think that no one can understand it; so you leave it lying around and someone finds it, gives it to the Security police who, I reckon, can decode most things very easily. If something is in plain words, you tend to keep it safely hidden.'

Jeremy was nearly laughing; the simplicity of the professional's answer pleased him. 'Bad luck, Arthur – the expert has spoken,' he said and Arthur, a little embarrassed at having asked the question, smiled back.

Soon afterwards the four visitors left, one after the other, five minutes or so apart, one from the back, two from the front, one from the back. Three nights later, Stevens, in his big old-fashioned car, drove to meet Jeremy and Quick near Jeremy's flat; and together they recruited Quick as the sixth member of the group, the member who would deal with liaison and information and nothing else. It was not that his pacifism was a pose; it was simply that he had begun to call himself one because he had been able to find no other way of coming to terms with the violence which he knew that he was capable of. It had started for him at school when he had realized that he could not only win most fights that he got involved in but that he could enjoy hurting his opponents; so, being the boy he was, he had stopped fighting – it had not really been a conscious decision, it had simply seemed necessary at the time. He could not settle his own mind by being violent; so he had made up his mind that society could not settle its problems in warfare or revolution. But, as he grew up and as he saw more and more what actually happened in his country, he began to find that what his intellect told him and what his feelings had decided were a long way apart. The paradox, he decided, could not be resolved; what suited him as an individual and what society needed simply diverged – and because he was involved in society he could not declare pacifism as a panacea for all insoluble social ills. Revolution might be necessary sometimes; war might be necessary; but he himself would not fight, if only because he might turn out too effective a warrior.

So when Stevens offered him a job in an organization which, although it used violence, did not intend to use it against people, and a job, moreover, which could have been designed to suit his own paradox, allowing him to be both committed to changing society and able to hold to his personal resolve of not allowing himself violence, he did not really hesitate before he accepted. In a way he had, he decided, taken the decision a long time before.

4

Soon after Quick was recruited, Jeremy moved from his flat to a cottage nearer the University – it was, he announced to his friends, an incredible find, a converted stable which belonged to two old ladies who lived in the big Cape-Dutch house which the stable had once served – the cottage was set at the bottom of the long narrow garden, cut off from view of the house by a mass of unkempt trees and shrubs, and had a separate entrance which led into a small, unmade, and tree-lined lane. Its two big rooms and a kitchen and bathroom were enough for two or even three people; but its whitewashed walls of thick rough stone and its stone floors suited Jeremy's puritan conscience. The cottage was too expensive for Jeremy on his own, however, for naturally he refused to take any money from his parents and paid his way through University by doing private tutorial work; so he looked around for someone among his friends to share with him – but, delightful though the cottage was, no one seemed very happy to move in; partly it was that, though the cottage would be pleasant in summer, it might be bad in winter; partly it was that, since there were only two main rooms, and since Jeremy insisted on having one as bedroom and one as living-room, either the sharer would have to sleep in Jeremy's bedroom or would have to sleep in the living-room – and all Jeremy's friends knew that he did not sleep much and that to sleep in the living-room would mean that you shared Jeremy's hours. Partly it was that, though many admired Jeremy and some even loved him, no one was eager to test that love by living with him.

For a time it seemed that Sheilagh Owen, who was not Jeremy's girl but the nearest person to being it, might live there with him – but then, because her professor at the University heard that she might, she was discreetly warned that it would be considered behaviour not fitting to a lady student of the University. Jeremy was really quite relieved and said as much, even to Sheilagh – he liked Sheilagh; she was, he said, a tough and sensible girl, remarkably aware of politics; but he knew that the kind of life he needed to live left him no time for a serious sexual life. So, in the end, it was Quick who moved in, Quick who for five years had lived in a single room in the basement of a house in Sea Point, a room which, he said, was more or less permanently damp and in winter sometimes submerged.

Quick knew within a month that he had made a mistake – it was not that he grew any less fond of Jeremy but that he found the whole arrangement whereby he slept on a couch in the sitting-room and Jeremy had the bedroom to himself utterly inconvenient. Jeremy went to bed late and got up early; Quick went to bed late too but he got up late – he didn't have to be in his editorial office until noon and since he worked until eight each night he liked to think that he needed to sleep in the mornings. So when he found himself being woken at eight in the morning by Jeremy's sitting at the desk in the living-room and banging away at his typewriter he became very irritable; and after four mornings of this told Jeremy that either Jeremy would have to move his desk into the bedroom or else they would have to share bedrooms. Jeremy refused to move his desk – he could not, he said, bear working in the room in which he slept – so Quick moved his bed into Jeremy's room, with the wardrobes arranged so that the room was more or less divided into two.

But that too didn't work for long, Quick found. One night Jeremy, who had gone to a meeting at the University, came back a little earlier than expected to find, asleep in the bedroom and naked after making love, Quick and Mary.

They didn't wake up until Jeremy left the house. He banged the half-glass front door so hard that a pane shattered; and they woke up properly only when he banged the heavy garden gate too. They didn't know exactly what had happened but when, at midnight, Quick came back from dropping Mary at the University residence, he found Jeremy back in the flat, raging.

'What the bloody hell do you mean by doing that?' he shouted at Quick.

'Doing what?'

'Behaving like that in my bedroom.'

'Good heavens, man, it's half my bedroom – and anyway what's it to do with you?'

'I came in and found you both naked there.'

'What did you expect? That we made love in full evening dress?'

'You knew I was coming back.'

'Not as early as you did, if it was you who broke the front door – you said after midnight.'

'That's immaterial; I just don't like your using my bedroom like a whorehouse.'

'What on earth do you mean, like a whorehouse? I was making love to Mary. Good God, why this sudden rush of puritan blood?'

Jeremy's temper was gone already; 'O hell,' he said, 'I'm, sorry, Donald, but it just upset me. I just don't like it – not that you sleep with Mary but that it should happen in the bedroom.'

Quick was not mollified. 'Do you want me to make love to her here in the sitting-room?' he asked.

'No, of course not. But can't you go somewhere else?'

'Why the hell should we? I pay half the rent of this place, don't I?'

'Yes, you do. But can't you see that I can't go on living here if you don't accept what I ask about this?'

Jeremy's distress was so obvious to Quick that he had to accept – so it was agreed, not in so many words but as a convention, that Quick would not make love to Mary in the cottage. When he told her this, he expected her to be upset: but she did not seem to be, saying only, 'We'll have to find other places then.' So Quick said to her, 'But don't you think it's strange that Jeremy should behave so absurdly? I mean, it's almost unnatural, isn't it?'

'No,' she replied, 'I suppose it's natural.'

'But if I walked into a room and saw you naked I'd be excited, not furious.'

'Perhaps Jeremy's furious because he was excited.'

'Oh, don't be a sophist. I tell you, he's behaving almost as if he were queer.'

'Oh now you come off it – he's never shown the slightest sign of being queer, he goes out with girls, and I'm sure that he sleeps with Sheilagh.'

'Not in the cottage, he doesn't – he doesn't like it in the cottage.'

'The cottage is his home, after all – he hasn't got any other place to go to. You've always got your parents' home.'

'But I can't take you there to make love to you.'

'You know what I mean.'

'The fact is that I pay for half the cottage – I live there.'

'Well, if you won't agree, you'll just have to move, won't you?'

Quick could not answer; he had agreed, he knew, but he had not expected Mary to take Jeremy's side in this – he knew that he did not want to move. He liked Jeremy, he enjoyed the cottage much of the time, and now that the organization was beginning to get going, it was useful for Jeremy and him to share.

But that too created its own problems; particularly, the continual presence of Hunter at the cottage annoyed Quick. Try as he might, he could not help disliking Hunter. He did not mind Devis, because he could sense that Jeremy did not entirely trust him; but Hunter seemed to have a way through to Jeremy that he could not share. He saw how important Hunter's professional skills were to the organization, yet there was a part of him that reacted against the trained soldier, reacted against what he thought the man's political *naïveté*, reacted against the simplicity which Hunter seemed to find at the centre of every problem, even when he was being most intelligent. Quick himself was the kind of man who had to believe in the difficult, who had to believe that, if there were two ways of saying much the same thing, the harder way was probably the most accurate, even if it was less communicative. He knew that he was as intelligent as Hunter was; but his own intelligence was so completely different, so much more difficult in its processes, that he could not stomach what he called Hunter's *reductio ad simplicitiam*; and, since

Quick was usually on the defensive about his own intelligence, he would often tell Jeremy that Hunter's was not intelligence, it was shrewdness, cunning, something like that, something which should not be confused with true intelligence.

Whenever Hunter was in the cottage, Quick felt somehow that he should not be there – he had an impression that Hunter wanted to exclude him from Jeremy, even that Jeremy did not want him around when Hunter and he were talking. He would have understood that if they had been talking about something which they could not let him hear, say, about the technical side of the organization's workings; but they never discussed that in the cottage, they talked of other things, of soldiering, which Quick despised, of revolutionary tactics, which Quick thought premature, of international politics, in a way which Quick did not believe in and of other people in a way which Quick thought inhuman. Sometimes he would try to argue with them; but they seemed to listen to what he had to say for only as long as he was actually talking and then immediately they would go back to their own conversation, as though Quick had not spoken at all, as though what he had said was so obvious that it did not deserve any thought at all.

Yet Quick did not mind very much that Jeremy ignored him when others were there; in a way, he expected it. He understood that Jeremy had to keep each of his friendships separate, that he could not bear to have only one person in orbit around him at any particular time, that he needed to try to dominate each relationship, that he was bound to resent the obtrusion of a third person. It was Hunter who Quick resented; it was Hunter who Quick thought was trying to exclude him from Jeremy's company.

Once, he taxed Jeremy with this. 'Why does Hunter always seem to resent whatever I have to say when the three of us are talking?' he asked Jeremy.

'Oh, I don't think he resents you,' said Jeremy. 'I just think that he feels that you are on such a different wave-length to him that he can't completely understand you.'

'But he doesn't feel that with you? You don't feel that with him?'

'No, I can get on the same wave-length as him; and I can talk to you, but not at the same time really – you are such different people, you two. You like to talk about central problems, Hunter has made up his mind to ignore most of those, he's only interested in the things he thinks can be sorted out. You don't really want answers, he does – that's the difference.'

That was not enough for Quick; he could not accept that he did not have the same ability as Jeremy to move from one level of talk to another and, although he was flattered that Jeremy should think that he always went to the centre of the problem, he did not wish to be thought of as an impractical man, he did not wish to be the theorist always.

There was always this and other conflicts. There was the intellectual conflict on Quick's own level of big questions without necessary answers; there was the conflict over women that both had to admit but that neither entirely understood; and there was the conflict over whether it was necessary to be secretive. But Quick gradually realized that all these were symptoms rather than causes, that these were subsidences in the soil that were created by a deeper restlessness. He began to understand that there was always going to be something that would keep them apart, that there was something that would always make it necessary, when either tried to cross the shifting sand, that Jeremy or he must leap backwards and apart again to sure ground.

At first, Quick decided that the fault was simple; while he loved his family and was secure in its security, Jeremy, however much he tried, could not love his. Later still, Quick began to see that his own family love was not simply strength and Jeremy's family hatred was not simply weakness; and that being so, what made each so anxious to be friends, even to love each other, was that shifting sand itself.

Quick's mother had died when he was very young and his father, a schoolmaster, had married again soon afterwards – yet he had never resented his step-mother, not even when she had her son, Peter, after nearly eighteen years of marriage; she hadn't become his mother, she had always been his step-mother, but he loved her very much.

He had moved away from home as soon as he had started working, when he was seventeen, and he didn't talk very much about them; he didn't need to, any more than he needed to be secret about them – he used to go home almost every week, but there was never any question that he had to go home, for if he did not or could not go for a month his father and step-mother would greet him with just the same casual warmth. He had never had to rebel against home, never even had to state his independence from home, because it had never been a clinging home; and Quick knew that this gave him one kind of strength, for, although he needed the security of his home, he had never had to test the security; it was just there, the knowledge that whatever happened there was always some place that he would be taken in and welcomed.

Jeremy's family was, as all his friends knew, different; everybody knew that it was unhappy, that Mr Jeremy was, though a moderately successful businessman – he was managing director of a small company which sold coal, not to private consumers, but to other companies – a weakling, a beautiful man but weak, dominated by his wife who had been, once, his secretary and who now, still, kept a close and shrewd eye on the company; everybody knew the story of Jeremy's rebellion; everybody knew what the Judge had said to Mrs Jeremy when he had rescinded his Order that her son was to live at home; and everybody knew that Jeremy never went home if he could help it.

Quick had found all that out long before he moved into the cottage; but after living there for two months he found out that it wasn't that Jeremy did not love his mother. He decided that you really could not choose to love or to hate your parents, though you could try to reject their love as Jeremy had tried – but that didn't change the fact of love, even if it needed Court Orders to prove itself. So, when Jeremy had chosen to leave home, to defy their love and his own love, it changed only what he thought of himself, not what he thought of them – for he loved them both but he loved them separately, his mother as herself, his father as himself, but never as a pair. So, thought Quick, Jeremy must have tried to pretend that love was impossible – if he tried to love a woman, she would eat him up just as his mother had eaten his father; and if he tried to love a man, he would become like his mother, all-devouring. So, thought Quick, it was a classic case: a boy whose mother was able, powerful, loving, all the right male characteristics, and whose father was weak, gentle, a beautiful old man, almost a saint if you forgot that most saints were toughs, and so he loved his mother and loved his father but the wrong way round.

But that wasn't enough; and Quick knew that it failed to account for Jeremy. He was not simply a weakling, he was strong; and his strength came as much from the unhappiness as his weakness did; he was not a homosexual, his sexuality was tortured and obscure but it was not perverted – and that last might be as much caused by the mixing of a South African puritan with the old Adam as by any family unhappiness. Oh, the explanation might go part of the way; Quick knew that you could say that Jeremy extended his rebellion against his parents into a rebellion against society – you could say, just as well, that Quick himself had substituted a rebellion against society for a rebellion against his parents. It was not the contradiction that made nonsense of the explanation; it was that it left too much out. It left out all that existed outside personality, the facts of society and, in the end, the fact of love itself.

But however much Quick tried to understand, it did not make it any easier for him to go on sharing the cottage with Jeremy. The longer he lived there, the more often he found his anger at Jeremy's unhappiness unbearable – for it was anger, anger that Jeremy should allow his mother's love to pursue him into every corner, anger that Jeremy should not recognize what he was allowing to happen to him, and anger that Jeremy should have so little understanding of his own condition. Then he met Mrs Jeremy and it became worse because it became more complicated.

It happened one Sunday when Jeremy was away for the week-end, staying with family friends up the coast. Quick was lying on the lawn in front of the cottage, half-asleep in the sun, pretending to read. She must have come very quietly because he didn't know that she was there until she said, 'I am sorry to interrupt your peaceful Sunday.' Quick rolled over on to his back and, shading his eyes, looked at her; she was so obviously Jeremy's mother that he nearly laughed – not simply the features, the long line of the jaw softened by the large slightly loose mouth, the high-bridged and fine nose, the deep-set eyes, but the stance too, her whole way of holding herself, the square shoulders pugnacious, the tilt of the head scornful. 'Won't you sit down, Mrs Jeremy?' he said and she laughed, 'Is it so obvious?' and sat down on the lawn, letting herself unfold, very gracefully, on to the grass; Quick hadn't meant her to sit on the grass; and he protested but she was content to sit there – she wanted to sit in front of her son's house.

'Jeremy's not here, I'm afraid,' said Quick.

'I know.' She smiled at him. 'Really, Mr Quick (it is Mr Quick, isn't it?), do you think that I am so foolish that I'd come to see where my son lived while he was actually here? The only way I can see him now is by pretending to take no notice of him; then he may possibly come to see me, say once a month, once every two months.'

Quick hadn't expected anything like that; it was the kind of honesty which he longed for Jeremy to have. But it was so unexpected that he couldn't talk to her, so he said instead, 'Would you like to see the cottage?'

'Yes,' she said, standing up. 'I'd love to.'

Quick took her inside to show her the living-room, the kitchen, the divided bedroom. He found himself telling her as if she had been his own mother how difficult it was living there sometimes – he didn't tell her any of the big things, for that would have been a disloyalty, but he talked about the small inconveniences and he didn't worry that she looked at everything, in Jeremy's wardrobe, at his books, that she even made her son's bed which he had left unmade in his haste to be off the morning before. Then Quick offered her coffee and they took chairs and sat on the lawn and talked as if they were old friends – but not a word was said about Jeremy until she was about to leave. She was standing at the gate which led into the lane behind the cottage and she turned suddenly to him to say, 'Thank you for showing me the cottage, Donald.'

'Come whenever you like.'

'I wish I could. But I'd better not come when he's here unless he invites me,' and she smiled as she said this; but Quick knew that Jeremy smile and knew that what she said was as calculated.

'Shall I tell Jeremy you came?' he asked.

'Why do you all call him Jeremy? Not James.' Quick thought that he knew but he could not tell her. 'Is it because I call him James? Is that why? Do you really think that I'm the all-devouring mother?' and she laughed as she said this, as though laughter would take the hurt out of it. 'Oh, I shouldn't ask you that – you're his friend, aren't you, you're on his side.'

'There aren't any sides in this, Mrs Jeremy.'

'Yes, I know. I must go. Good-bye.' And she walked away down the lane, very elegant, very straight, without looking back.

Quick didn't mention to Jeremy that she had been; he could not face what he thought would be the inevitable questions. What had she done? What had she looked at? What had she said? Why had she come? So he planted the first lie in his row of lies and, when Jeremy asked who had made his bed, Quick pretended that he had done it himself, in a fit of philanthropy.

The second time she came, two months later, Jeremy was there. He and Quick were sitting in the front room, drinking coffee, and trying to work out why the cottage seemed to be costing them so much. When she knocked at the front door, they both looked up and saw who it was. Quick waited for Jeremy to get up to let her in; but when Jeremy didn't move he got up himself and opened the door.

'Hullo,' he said.

'Hullo, Donald. Hullo, James.' Jeremy didn't move from his chair and all he said was, 'I didn't know that you knew Quick.' She looked at Quick and knew that she had made a mistake. So she smiled and said, 'Oh, we met one day when I came here to try to see you.' Damn her, thought Quick; now he'll know.

'You didn't tell me.' Jeremy's voice accused Quick.

'Oh, I must have forgotten. I was half-asleep, wasn't I, Mrs Jeremy?' She had to agree. She was still standing, Jeremy was still sitting, and he made no sign to welcome her. So Quick offered her a chair and asked if she would like a glass of wine or a cup of coffee, but she would not even sit down. She stood in front of her son, and, seeming not to care that Quick was in the room, or perhaps, he thought, despising him, said, 'You know, James, I haven't seen you for four months.'

'I've been busy,' he replied.

'Too busy to call in even for five minutes?'

He didn't reply; Quick decided that he should go and started to move towards the bedroom. 'Don't go, Donald,' said Jeremy. 'I don't think my mother's staying long.'

'No, I can't stay. I really came to tell you, James, that your father was ill – it's his birthday on Tuesday too and I thought you might come to see him.'

There was no life in Jeremy's voice when he replied, asking what was wrong with his father.

'Oh nothing really,' said Mrs Jeremy. 'He's been working too hard and is tired. Will you come?'

'I'll try and come on Tuesday.'

'For dinner?'

'Probably not for dinner. I'll come after dinner.'

'At about nine?'

'Yes, about then.'

'Promise?' She couldn't help herself, she had to say that, Quick knew. It was part of her, that need to have everything promised – she could not take any kind of love on trust.

'No, I won't promise,' said Jeremy. 'I said I'd try to come on Tuesday.'

'Please try not to forget, James. Will you remind him, Donald?'

'I'll try to,' Quick said – he wished he could get out of the room; it was very hot there, as though suddenly a summer storm had blown up out of nothing but a wisp of cloud. Jeremy got up from his chair. He did not look at his mother. The hair over his forehead was wet with sweat. His tie was crooked, the knot pulled over under the collar. As he stood there, his mother reached out, as any mother might, to straighten his tie; and as she put her hand out, Jeremy jumped backwards to avoid having her touch even his clothes. It wasn't hatred that made him do it, Quick knew; not even hatred could create such revulsion.

At that moment Quick realized that he could not go on living in the same house as Jeremy, that he could not tolerate such unhappiness for another moment. It would not matter so much if he could be away from it sometimes; if he could limit his attempt to cope with it to times that he was able to cope with it, he could go on being friends with Jeremy; but he could not live with it. It would destroy him in just the same way that he believed that it was destroying Jeremy.

But though he had taken the decision he did not say anything to Jeremy or to Mary immediately – he wanted to find a reason for going that would not hurt Jeremy too much. So, quite deliberately, he waited until a night that he knew Jeremy would be home and then he brought Mary back to the cottage; for a while the three of them sat and talked, Jeremy swivelled round in the chair at his desk, Mary and Quick close together on the sofa and Jeremy and Mary talked well and wittily and wisely and Quick sat quiet, knowing what had to be done. Gradually he began to behave more and more sensually towards Mary, touching her hair, stroking her arms, kissing the back of her neck, and gradually he could sense Jeremy's retreating, going back into himself until finally he said, 'I must get back to my work, if you don't mind.' Usually at that stage Quick would take Mary away but tonight he didn't – he took her by the hand and led her into the bedroom and there began to make love to her, deliberately provoking all her sexuality, deliberately forcing her not to care what Jeremy thought, not to care that he knew what was happening, that he could hear what was happening. She protested at first, whispering, 'But what about Jeremy?' but soon she submitted – and Quick went on, deliberately, until he heard Jeremy leave the cottage; when, knowing that he had won, he brought Mary to her climax and pretended to reach his own too.

Two hours later, when he came back from dropping Mary at the university, Jeremy was again at his desk. For a moment or two, Quick thought that perhaps it hadn't worked, for Jeremy said nothing at all, simply went on banging at his typewriter; but then he suddenly tore the page out of it, crumpled it up, hurled it at the floor and said, 'Why did you do that, Donald? What were you trying to do?'

'What are you talking about?'

'You know bloody well. Did you do it deliberately? Were you deliberately trying to drive me out of my own home?'

'I don't know what you are talking about.'

'You do know.' Jeremy was raging now, his face white, his nostrils distended. 'You do know. Why did you do it?'

'If you are talking about why I made love to Mary, I don't think it is anything to do with you.'

'It is everything to do with me. This is my home and I will not have it destroyed.'

Now Quick knew again that he was right; he had to leave and this was the way it had to be done. There was no other way, he thought.

'It's my home too,' he said, 'and making love to Mary here means that it is my home.'

'It's not your home – you have a home. Why can't you leave it to me? Why must you dirty it?'

'What I was doing with Mary was not dirty and, if you think it was, there's something wrong with you.' Quick was cold still but he could feel the blood beating at the doors of his mind – he had to leave, he had to. And now Jeremy gave him the chance, for half-shouting, half-crying, he said, 'Then leave, damn you; get out of my home, stay away from my home.' The surrender was signed, Quick knew – he turned away, went through the kitchen, out of the back door, round the house, and he walked for three hours, blindly through the suburbs, until he knew that Jeremy must be asleep.

Next morning nothing was said; but when Quick got back to the cottage that evening, Jeremy spoke immediately – 'I'm terribly sorry about last night,' he said. 'I was overwrought. I know that I shouldn't get so worked up about you and Mary but it was just too much for me last night.' The sickness in his voice and eyes was such that Quick could not help saying, 'I'm sorry too, Jeremy. It was thoughtless of me. But I do think that I had better leave, don't you?'

'If you feel that you must, I suppose you'd better. I don't want you to go.'

'Don't you? You said last night. . . .'

'Nothing I said last night means anything. Do you know where I went last night?'

'You mean when you left because of me and Mary.'

'Yes.' Jeremy smiled. 'I suppose I behave idiotically at times. I went home.'

There was nothing that Quick could say. Jeremy went on, 'I hadn't been there the whole time you've been living here, you know. The only time I've seen my mother was that time she came here.'

'What happened there last night?'

'Nothing. Nothing out of the ordinary. It was just terrible.' He smiled again, not quite looking at Quick. 'Does that sound silly? It was just as terrible as it has ever been. And nothing happened at all.' He looked up at Quick, looked straight at him staring straight into the eyes of whatever darkness he saw. 'Do you really have to leave?'

'Yes,' said Quick. 'I must leave.'

'Even if I tell you that I need you?'

For a moment Quick wondered what terrible beast it was that he had let free, what beast, quite separate from him or Jeremy or Mary or Jeremy's mother or Stevens or anybody, was walking through the cottage and down the back lane and round the suburbs of Cape Town. But he could not change his mind, he had to leave, so he said, 'You don't need me.'

'Don't you understand, Donald? I need you here, I need to have you living here.'

'No, you don't need anyone – you don't need me, or Sheilagh, or anyone.' He could not mention who was most important of all.

'Leave Sheilagh out of this.'

'You can't leave her out of this. If you don't realize how much she loves you you must be blind. And that's part of the same thing.'

'Talk about you, not Sheilagh. Why's it the same thing?'

'Because you say that you need us and what you mean is that you want to own us without owing us anything – you want us here, you want us around you, but you won't give us anything.'

'I've given you a lot, Donald – I've given you half my home –

and this is my home, it isn't just lodgings; you have somewhere to go, I don't – and I've given you complete trust.'

'What kind of trust?'

'Enough trust for you to send me to gaol for a very long time.'

'And that's all we share, isn't it? The threat that we hold over each other.'

'I've never threatened you with it.'

'Oh God, Jeremy, this is completely pointless. It's simply that I can't go on living here – it isn't that I've become your enemy or that I hate you; I just can't live here.'

'Is it because what happened with my mother? Is it that?'

'It's nothing to do with anybody except me – it's inside me. I can't live here.'

'Even if I tell you again that I need you?'

'I've given you the answer to that already.'

'You can't ever answer for what is inside me,' said Jeremy. Quick knew that there was nothing more that could be said; but he was still fixed in his purpose to leave and Jeremy seemed to realize this for he said nothing more that night and the next day they discussed Quick's going as if it had been normally decided. Within a fortnight Quick was gone from the cottage.

For a time Jeremy stayed on; he did not seem to look for anyone to share with him and nobody knew how he managed to pay the rent. After a month or two he started to sublet the cottage for a few days at a time while he went to sleep in friends' spare rooms or on floors or, once or twice, in a sleeping-bag on a beach. Then it seemed that he was virtually living with Sheilagh, who had given up her room at the University residence and had a bed-sitting room in Mowbray, for he sublet the cottage for two months to a visiting lecturer from the U.S.A. In the end, however, he gave up the lease entirely and took a small flat near where his old flat in Wynberg had been. Few people outside the group were sure where his new rooms were; he never seemed to ask anyone to go there and usually met his friends in Sheilagh's room.

Quick and Jeremy did not stop being friends. For a time Quick felt such a guilt at having left the cottage that he could hardly bear to meet Jeremy. But the work for the organization went on; and they had the same friends; and after that one evening Jeremy seemed not to care that Quick had left; and so Quick began to think that he had done right in getting out. Certainly, Sheilagh seemed happier; Jeremy was always with her and seemed content that they should be treated as a couple. But if the friendship went on, neither made any effort to cross the shifting sand between them; it was simply a friendship like any other friendship. They were, to put it another way, down from the mountains.

5

The organization prospered; oh, but they were good, oh, they were bloody good at their work. There were, admittedly failures – first Hunter refused to wait beyond the exact time set for the rendezvous and so, when the second car arrived ten minutes late, the operation had to be called off. At the post-mortem meeting held as Quick had planned it, though he had not been involved in the operation itself, Jeremy immediately launched into an attack on what he called Hunter's unreasonableness – 'Surely you knew,' he demanded from Hunter. 'Surely you knew that we were coming? Surely you could have guessed that anything might have held us up? A puncture, the car's not starting, something minor like that?'

'We agreed to meet at 1.35 exactly; I waited until 1.40 and then left. You were at fault, not me.'

'Yes, Hunter's right – you might have been stopped by the cops or anything. . . .' Devis defended too, though Jeremy and Roseman knew that he, in the first car with Hunter, had wanted to wait longer. Still Jeremy was not satisfied, for he broke into Devis's defence as it was tailing off, 'Oh, Arthur, don't be a fool – there was nothing in our car to make us a danger; you and Hunter had the materials in yours.'

'Yes,' Hunter said patiently, 'and we were there on time. You were not. The circumstances are immaterial – if anyone is not exactly in his place at the right time, nothing is to go forward.'

'All right, Hunter,' Jeremy answered, 'I know all about your professional standards. But surely this was just silliness, not waiting five minutes for the second car?'

'This is not a game we're playing,' said Hunter.

Now Jeremy was defending: 'Yes, not a game, but we've got to understand, even though some of us are more trained than others, that this whole business is just a start; and we are bound to take time to learn.'

'No – this is professional. And though you may sneer at what you called my "professional standards", we simply can't afford to take time to learn. There are no trainee saboteurs. There are live ones and there are dead ones. There can't be any mistakes. We had planned the operation fully and should have been there.' Hunter's voice had lost the military edge for a moment – he was simply a passionately concerned man and every person in the room knew that he was right. But now he became the military man again, with what sounded to Jeremy like some formula – 'If anyone is not exactly in his place at the right time, nothing is to go forward.'

So Roseman tried to play the reasonable man; 'Look, Hunter,' he said, 'we accept that you're right. But don't say simply that we can't take time to learn. For example, you put us in the second car in danger last night – we waited half an hour for you. What would we have said if the police had asked us what we were doing there?' Before Hunter could reply, Jeremy had answered Roseman; 'Oh, hell, Raymond, what danger could we have been in? We had nothing in the car. We could have told any curious policeman anything, that we were admiring the view, having a sleep before driving home, anything.' The others could feel his anger with Roseman; and Devis at least was sure that he knew the reason – that Roseman had been responsible for the second car's lateness.

But Devis was wrong; Jeremy had been at fault. For just a few minutes when Roseman had arrived at the cottage to fetch him, Jeremy had found himself unable to go through with the plan; oh, he had not shown it, not even to Quick who had been there and who knew what was happening that night, not even to Roseman. He had had to leave Roseman waiting outside the cottage, had had to send Quick out to tell him that he would not be a moment, and he had hidden himself in the bathroom. At first he had thought that he was simply going to be sick – he had leaned over the basin and had tried to retch. But he could not be sick and, as he stood up, he knew what was wrong was not simply fear, because fear alone he was used to. What was wrong came from something else, came from the bones and shadows of the face that he looked at in the mirror; he had looked into his own reflected eyes and all he had seen there had been himself looking into his own reflected eyes and he had known that, if he could see small enough, the same pattern of eye repeating reflected eye would be there, like some darkness that he could not find his way in. If I were so big, he thought, that all I could see in this mirror was the reflection of just one of my eyes, would I see still the same repeated eyes? Or would I see other people there too, hundreds of people, jabbering, sneering, waving their arms, waving flags, crying out, 'We see you, we see you'? And if I could see other people there, who would they be? Would they all just be me doing different things? Or would they be people I knew? Or people I had never seen? And if I don't know that, he had thought, how can I know who I'm doing this for? Am I doing it for all those other people whom I don't know, or am I doing it for just those hundreds of other Jeremy-people who would jump up and down, some shouting yes and some shouting no? And then he had looked closer and had seen that the face in the mirror was crying, not moving as a face should when it is crying, but just very still, not looking at anything at all, crying, and he had put his hands up to his face and had been almost surprised to find that he was crying himself. Oh, you fool, he had said, oh you fool to cry – you took this decision a long time ago; you had the choice and you made it and there is no going back now. But still the face had cried; and then suddenly there were more faces in the mirror and all of them were crying, and he knew that they were all crying for him, that they were all Jeremy-people, that he was crying for himself. And that he knew was terrible, not only for him to cry for himself, but for all those others to cry for themselves too; then he had known that he would go.

That was why he'd been late, he knew; Roseman had cursed him when he arrived at the car but they had not been able to catch up the lost time, for Roseman would not exceed the speed limits at all – 'We are late,' he had said, 'but we can't afford to be caught for speeding – that would be worse than being late; anyway, it will only be fifteen minutes.' But it had been less than fifteen minutes, it had been only ten, and then the first car had not been there as it should have been and they had been able to curse Hunter and Devis until they began to think that perhaps they were not coming and then, later, that perhaps they had not waited. Jeremy had not been afraid then; and it made him sure that it had not been fear that had held him in the cottage, unable to go out to Roseman and the already taken decision; he had made Roseman stay on and on, first fifteen minutes, then twenty, then thirty, before he had agreed that they should wait no longer.

Now, while the argument between Hunter, Roseman, and Devis went tediously on, he had had enough. He signed to Stevens that he thought that the argument was pointless and Stevens, as chairman, broke in to stop it and to suggest that, now that it was accepted that operational meetings had to be exactly on time, the best thing they could do was to plan the next operation. At the end of the meeting, Jeremy went up to Hunter and said, 'You were quite right, Hunter. I was late and I should not have been. I'm sorry. I was a little late at the cottage. I was frightened, I suppose. I am sorry.' He was surprised at Hunter's reaction which was to smile and say, 'So was I frightened – and I don't suppose, I know. But we really can't afford to make mistakes.'

'I thought professionals would stop being afraid,' Jeremy said. It seemed easier to talk of fear than of the other more difficult thing.

'No, they don't – what happens to some of them is that it becomes like a drug, that they actually need the fear, that without it they feel that they are not really functioning as they should.'

'Do you find it very difficult working with amateurs like us?' Jeremy said.

'No,' was Hunter's again surprising reply. 'I prefer it. It is like I wasn't a professional any more. You see, you people are doing this not because it is your job to do it; you are doing it because you believe in it. It makes a great difference.' Once more Jeremy was struck by the almost naïve quality of the man's intelligence – yet it was intelligence, there was no doubt of that; and it was honesty too, the kind of honesty that only *naïveté* was capable of. Jeremy found himself feeling suddenly that this man was the best of all of them; he was a frightening man because he was so sure of what he was doing but Jeremy, who knew what effort it took to achieve the look of certainty, decided that Hunter must fight for certainty as anyone had to fight.

From that moment on there seemed to be no more trouble between Hunter and Jeremy and, where before Stevens had found himself growingly worried about the splits that existed in the group, between Roseman and himself on the one side, Jeremy and his protégés Devis and Quick on another, and Hunter, who Stevens was sure was the most important person in the group, at least for a long time yet, he realized now that Jeremy and Hunter had come together. Jeremy began to accept that Hunter knew, technically and professionally, more than anyone in the group and that his leadership there must be assumed – but Hunter, in his turn, began to treat Jeremy as a leader, as the experienced sergeant in a platoon might accept a young and inexperienced officer. This of course left Stevens and Roseman out of Jeremy's circle; but Stevens knew that Jeremy must accept his leadership in some things and he knew that he and Roseman were close enough together to force Jeremy not to treat the group as his personal offspring and, as importantly, to ensure that Roseman would not act without consulting Stevens first. Still, as Stevens was forced to recognize, if the group ever found itself faced with a crisis of leadership, Jeremy had replaced him as the natural leader; he was not altogether worried about this, for he had not seen himself except as the initial leader – by temperament and habit he was not an activist, he liked to start things and to give them a push sometimes if they seemed to be dying, but he preferred his own thoughts to guiding the thoughts of others. Roseman, he thought, would be the only trouble; for, if Roseman found Stevens giving up leadership entirely to Jeremy, he might grow dissatisfied – but Jeremy, he thought, was just as capable as he was of recognizing that Roseman was becoming a little the odd man out of the group and so he would make sure that he did not altogether lose Roseman.

In this Stevens was completely correct for, soon afterwards, Roseman suggested that the present system of pairing for operations might be altered so that Jeremy went with Hunter and

Devis with him. But Jeremy would not have this; nor would Devis, since if he could not work with Jeremy as he would have liked to do, he preferred more to work with Hunter than with Roseman; and Hunter, too, argued that there was no need to change the present pairs, since they had not yet had the chance to try them out.

It was a lapse in Hunter's own professional standards which caused the failure of the second expedition. The rendezvous had taken place exactly on time – this time, Hunter and Devis had driven to a point five miles out of Cape Town, on the main road to Stellenbosch – there, they had waited until 11.30, when Roseman and Jeremy, carrying the material in their car, had passed them. The second car had followed the first for another mile, keeping well behind, and had then followed the first off on to a small side road leading into the bush. After going a mile down this, the first car had stopped, Devis had stayed behind with it – he opened up the bonnet as if something were wrong with the engine and so that he could stop any car that followed – and Hunter had transferred to Roseman's car. Half a mile further down the road, Roseman had dropped Hunter and Jeremy with the material; then he had driven another half-mile up the road and had then stopped to wait. Hunter and Jeremy had walked a few hundred yards off the road to a small electricity substation which they set to blow in about three hours' time. They had then returned to the road, where they were picked up by Roseman, taken back to Devis's car where Hunter was dropped, and then the two cars made their way back to Cape Town separately. It was child's work, as Devis said to Hunter when they were driving back to town.

There was no news in the paper next day; and Quick told Jeremy that he had not heard a whisper of any news about sabotage, not even any news that the police had found something that they were trying to hush up. On the Tuesday a short paragraph said only that three officers of the Anti-Sabotage squad of the Security police had been called to dismantle charges found in an electricity substation outside Cape Town. 'The police are investigating the incident and expect to make arrests shortly,' the report said; but Quick passed on the news that he had heard that the police did not really think that arrests were likely. Three days later another paragraph said that three Africans had been arrested in connection with the incident; but no charges were laid although no report was ever published that they had been released. Then Quick, who had been made anxious by the arrests, found out that the Africans had in fact been released; and since Jeremy had said to him, 'Look, even if they were charged, there is nothing we could do – we can only avoid physical damage to people, we can't prevent the police punishing the innocent,' and since no one else in the group seemed worried, Quick did not press his private worry that those kind of unjust arrests were inevitable only because the group made them inevitable.

Any doubts, even Quick's, were removed by the success of the third operation. This time they had resolved, partly because of a suggestion by Stevens, partly because they were all anxious to make the existence of a new wave of sabotage publicly felt, to blow the signal lines of the main suburban railway, that which brought many of the white commuters into work from their homes along the coast, Simonstown, Glencairn, Fishhoek, St James, Muizenberg, False Bay and so on. This time Quick acted as distributor of the explosives and fuses, handing out to each member of the group from his car parked down a dark cul-de-sac in Rondebosch already made-up charges, set with half-hour fuses; Hunter placed his at Mowbray, Jeremy at Newlands, Devis at Wynberg, and Roseman at Rosebank, and all five of them were back in their beds by the time of the first explosion, at Mowbray.

Next morning, suburban traffic was in chaos – and Jeremy who, for fun, travelled into Cape Town that morning, had rare pleasure in joining his fellow-travellers on Wynberg station to curse the inefficiency of the railways and then, when he and three commuters hired a taxi to drive them the six miles into Cape Town – for Jeremy was enjoying his joke – to curse the reds who were intent on ruining private enterprise by disturbing the even tenor of business lives. Quick, coming home from work later that day, was less than amused when he discovered on Jeremy's desk a pile of cuttings from newspapers; but his pleasure at the success, particularly because his editor had sent him to write a follow-up story on the police investigations, was such that Jeremy's outburst of exhibitionism, even though it conflicted with his idea of Jeremy as a deeply secretive person, did not much disturb him. Devis, at the university, joined a group of his friends at a table in the refectory where he allowed himself even more inflammatory statements than usual, though he was careful to say that he had spent the night before in a drunken stupor from nine o'clock onwards. Roseman surprised his wife by phoning her during the morning to suggest that she met him for lunch in town; and only Hunter spent the day as he spent every day, working in the library.

But the wonder lasted not even nine days; and the two reactions which the group – or all the group but Hunter, who did not talk much of the future – had hoped for seemed not to happen; for Africans, if they reacted at all, were too wise to show it; and whites reacted not by talking of concessions but by demanding that the Government take action to ensure the efficiency of the police in preventing such sabotage. So the group had to decide to strike harder the next time, to strike at something the loss of which would mean more than temporary inconvenience to the country.

So because it had been a hot dry summer and the winter rains were delayed, the group decided to try to blow a reservoir. It was, they realized, likely to be a much more difficult job than the signal lines had been; for not only was a reservoir likely to be more difficult to get at but it presented, physically, a more difficult technical task. But Hunter thought that, even if the group could not manage to breach the dam wall, they could perhaps manage to destroy enough of a pumping station to make a reservoir impossible to operate for some time.

First, they had to find the right kind of reservoir – Cape Town and its suburbs are served by a good many; gradually the group visited one after the other and gradually one after the other was found to be impossible, until, one day, Jeremy told Hunter that he had found one which might be within their scope. It was a small reservoir, about twenty miles from Cape Town, away in the hills above Belville; it was used mainly to supplement the big reservoirs that served most of the Cape; and lying as it did in a natural valley, from which it took its name of the Helmet Reservoir, the wall seemed to be easier to blow than most of those they had looked at. What was as important was that it had only a small staff; for during the day a white maintenance engineer and two coloured workers looked after it and at night there was only a single African nightwatchman, whose hut lay some way from the wall and pumping house, a good hundred yards up the southern side of the dam.

Hunter went to see the dam and thought that they could manage it. He worked out that, if he mined the wall three times, twice at the base on the outside (as far as he could see from his necessarily casual investigation, there were two over-flow pipes down there which he could use as bases for these explosions) and once higher up the wall, on the inside, and then mined the small pumping house and its machinery, which stood on the southern side of the dam, on the edge of a plantation of eucalyptus trees, they could be almost certain of making the reservoir useless, even if they did not manage to breach the wall.

What was technically difficult was, first, the placing of the charges and, secondly, the timing of the explosions – for it seemed essential that the three explosions in the face of the wall itself should happen at exactly the same moment; as well, Hunter wanted the fourth charge, that in or next to the pumping house, to happen five minutes or so after the other explosions rather than simultaneously. He wanted this, he said, to make sure that the nightwatchman, if he was anywhere around, would have a chance to get away when he heard the first explosions. Roseman wanted to know what would happen if he did not move away, if he went instead to investigate – but Hunter and Jeremy pooh-poohed his concern, saying that the nightwatchman, since he was not likely to take a proprietary concern in the reservoir, would certainly run away when he heard the first explosion.

'What's the alternative, Raymond?' asked Jeremy. 'Blow the pumping house at the same time and just take the chance that the nightwatchman won't be near it?'

'We could watch to see that he doesn't go near,' suggested Roseman.

'Obviously,' said Hunter, 'we'll have to have someone watching him while we are laying the charges; because we won't be able to do it if he is around. But I'm prepared to bet that he doesn't move from his hut most nights.'

'We will have someone watching, then,' interrupted Roseman. He did not want Hunter to say anything that he might find offensive about how that was the way most Africans behaved, for Roseman believed that all generalizations of that kind were concealed racialism.

'Not all the time, we won't,' laughed Devis.

'Of course not,' said Jeremy. 'Whoever watches will have to get away at least in time for us to be clear before the explosions.'

'I understand that,' said Roseman; but he did not sound as if he were satisfied in his understanding so Stevens intervened. 'I understand your concern, Roseman,' he said. 'But I do think that what Hunter says is correct; if we are to blow this dam, we will have to do it that way; someone can watch the nightwatchman until just before the explosion – and I agree that the man is not likely to come down to investigate. He's more likely to run for help.'

'Isn't there a telephone there that he might use?' asked Roseman.

'I looked carefully,' said Hunter, who had, in fact, looked carefully for this, 'but there didn't seem to be any telephone wires leading either to the watchman's hut or to the pumping house.'

'I'm sure there's no need to worry, Roseman,' said Stevens. 'Though, of course, if you think that there is a real risk, we had better call this operation off.' But Roseman would not consider that, as Stevens had guessed he would not. So they agreed that the operation should go forward.

The next problem was that, using the simple burning fuses which they had used before, Hunter could not be sure that he could time the three explosions on the wall exactly enough; he would have to use, he said, a more complex timing mechanism. So Devis was sent to buy four alarm clocks from city stores – he got one from each of four main departmental stores, buying the most simply operated which he could find. Each of these Hunter turned, with the aid of four small electric torches, into electrically sensitive fuses. Attached to charges and with the timing set, all that had to be done was to set each alarm to go off at the same time and, instead of the alarm going, the fuse would be made active.

Hunter knew, too, that he could not be certain that the placing of the charges on the wall would actually weaken it enough for the weight of water to breach it – he was not an engineer and could not find a way of calculating whether the maximum charge he could set would be enough, or the placing accurate enough, to bring the wall down; but he thought that it might weaken the wall permanently, at the very least – the rest he had to hope for. At least it would be possible to damage the pumping house irreparably.

The four activists in the group did not pair off for this operation – Roseman was given the task of making sure that the nightwatchman did not come near while the other three were laying the charges; it would need three people, Jeremy to crawl along the top of the wall and lower down the inside of the wall a water-tight time-set charge, fixed on the end of a long piece of lightweight wire, Devis and Hunter to set the charges in the base of the wall, up the overflow pipes if possible; the last two were to wait until Jeremy whistled to show that he had completed his part and were then to set the timing mechanism on their charges to coincide with the explosion on the inside – Jeremy would have to carry an already time-set charge, since it would have to be made watertight in the car. It was not worthwhile, however, said Hunter, to set all four charges in the car, that would increase the risk unnecessarily. The fourth charge, that for the pumping house, Roseman was to carry and then leave for Jeremy and Hunter to fix after they had finished charging the wall.

As well, Hunter decided that since they would have to carry such a large quantity of explosive from Cape Town to the reservoir it would be best if one person was in charge of transport, to take the explosives from the garage where they were stored to near the reservoir in a single car – that way, the risk, if anything went wrong, would not be unnecessarily increased.

Hunter went through the plan of action on his own meticulously, again and again; simple though it was, he wanted to make sure that nothing could go wrong. Then, with Jeremy, Devis, and Roseman, he went through it again and again, until he was sure that they had the details of what had to be done and of what should be done if anything went wrong, if they were disturbed or if the nightwatchman was prowling. Particularly, he showed Jeremy, on a dummy charge, how to unseal it, open it up, and disconnect the fuse from the charge – he would, he said, set the charge himself but he had to know that Jeremy could disconnect it in an emergency. Then Hunter, with Jeremy to help him, set about building the charges and the fuses; and when that was done, they waited for the night they had chosen.

The meticulous plans paid off; on a Wednesday night, Devis drove a car-load of charges and fuses, each one, he chuckled to Jeremy, enough to blow him and his car on to the top of Table Mountain, to about half a mile from the reservoir. There, he met Hunter, Jeremy, and Roseman. Devis parked his car under the trees and they then transferred the charges and fuses to Hunter's Landrover and moved it up through the plantation until they were overlooking the reservoir. Roseman went off immediately to check the whereabouts of the nightwatchman, leaving Hunter to set the charges and fuses. After a few minutes Roseman was back to report that he could hear the nightwatchman talking to someone, a woman he thought, in his hut. Hunter then set and sealed Jeremy's charge, and while Hunter was checking the other three, Jeremy fixed his charge to a thirty-five foot length of thin pliable wire. When he was satisfied that it was firm and when Hunter had checked it, the four moved off, Hunter and Devis to make their way to the base of the wall, Jeremy and Roseman to the pumping house. When they reached it, Roseman left against the back wall of the pumping house the charge that he had been carrying and moved off towards the nightwatchman's hut.

Jeremy, waiting in the shadows of the pumping house, looked at his watch – he was to wait here three minutes; if no sound came from Roseman, he was to assume that all was well. Gradually the second hand jerked around; one, two, three minutes, no sound from Roseman, and it was time to go. He moved out quickly to the edge of the shadows and his eyes, used to the dark, picked out the dam wall easily; it was narrow but a railing along its outer edge made it seem secure. He was, according to Hunter's plan, to crawl out to the middle; but it seemed silly to do that, it was so dark, and Roseman was there to stop the nightwatchman if anything went wrong – so he simply walked out, one hand on the railing to guide him, the other holding the charge. When he reached what he judged was the middle of the wall, he stopped, knelt down, and tied the end of the wire firmly around the base of the railing. Then, very gently, he lowered the charge down into the water – it sank immediately, since Hunter and he had filled the empty parts of the water-tight container with dry sea-sand, and very soon the wire ran taut from the railing to the water. Jeremy stood up, leaned over the railings, and listened for a moment though it was a very quiet night, he could not hear any movement below. But Hunter and Devis must be there, he knew, so he whistled three times and heard, in reply, a double whistle from below. They must have moved quickly, he knew, to be ready so soon; he had expected a few moments' delay.

Jeremy walked quietly back along the wall to wait again in the shadow of the pumping house; there had still been no sound from or sight of Roseman, seventy yards or so up the bank. He would have to wait a few moments now for Hunter to come up from below the dam – Devis had been told to go straight back to his car and then home, without waiting for them. While he was waiting for Hunter, he tried the door of the pumping house – it seemed to be solidly locked. He took a small torch from his pocket and shone it up and down the door; there were heavy padlocks at the top and the bottom and Jeremy realized that they would probably have to fix the last charge to the outside of the pumping house. He looked for a place but before he had found one, Hunter arrived; he was panting from the climb from below the wall. Hunter had no trouble finding a place to fix the charge, choosing to do so where the pipes ran from the house to the water. Jeremy fetched the charge from the back of the house where Roseman had left it, Hunter fixed it to the joint of the pipes and the wall, set it, and stood up. Immediately Jeremy whistled three times, to tell Roseman that they were moving off – his double whistle in reply assured them that all was still well; now Roseman was to wait another four minutes, to give them time to get back to the Landrover, before he came to join them. Then they had about six minutes before the first explosion.

Neither Jeremy nor Hunter said much as they sat in the car waiting for Roseman to come; Jeremy said that Hunter and Devis had been very quick down below and Hunter told him that they had managed to use the overflow pipes as he had hoped – after Jeremy's whistle, they had set the fuses and then pushed the charges as far as they could up the dry overflow pipes, right into the middle of the wall, Hunter said. Then they sat quiet, waiting for Roseman – Hunter did not even look at his watch but Jeremy could not control his impatience, not to be off, but to know that the operation had been a success. Then Roseman came running back, moving quickly and quietly for such a large man; he opened the back door and jumped in and almost before the door was shut, Hunter had the Landrover moving out from the trees and on to the road.

'All right, Raymond?' called Jeremy from the front seat.

'Yes,' shouted Raymond, 'except for you.' He was still breathing so hard that he was difficult to hear.

'What?' shouted Jeremy.

'You,' shouted Roseman. 'Why didn't you crawl out as you were meant to? You walked – I could see you clearly against the skyline.'

'But surely . . .' answered Jeremy.

'Surely nothing,' said Hunter from next to him. He did not sound angry. 'I told you to crawl. I checked the skyline from near the watchman's hut and knew that you would be seen if you walked and didn't crawl.'

'Yes,' said Roseman. There was no need to shout now – the Landrover was off the unmade road and on the tarmac road leading to the main road. 'I could see you clearly as daylight. You walked out there, then disappeared, down below the skyline, and then you got up, leaned over the railings, whistled, and then walked back. If the nightwatchman had been out of his hut, he would have been bound to see you.'

'Was he in the hut all the time?' asked Hunter.

'Yes, fortunately,' said Roseman. 'I was right – he must have had a woman in there – the door was open and he had a coal fire in a bucket standing in the entrance and I could hear them talking and laughing. Christ, it's lucky he didn't come out.'

'I'm sorry,' said Jeremy. 'I didn't think of the skyline.'

'I should bloody well hope so,' said Roseman. He was very angry still, Jeremy could hear – it must have been bad out there, just sitting, waiting, and then watching Jeremy walking out and being able to do nothing and watching the door of the hut, expecting the man out at any moment.

But Hunter said nothing more, only, 'How's the time?'

Jeremy looked, then answered, 'Two minutes to go, I make it. Shall we stop and listen?'

'No,' said Hunter. 'No. We must get on.'

'It won't take a moment,' said Jeremy. 'Just pull off the road to listen.'

'No,' said Hunter. 'Dammit, I said no.'

So Jeremy did not hear either of the explosions – and next morning, when Quick opened his newspaper and saw the headline, SABOTEURS BLOW RESERVOIR, he was so delighted that he did not notice the subheading for a moment. It worked, he thought, it must have worked wonderfully – good for Hunter, he wasn't sure that it would work but it has, it has; but then he saw the subheading and suddenly shut the paper again, as if he hoped that his action would change what he had seen. Then he sat down on the sofa and opened the paper again. He read it quickly twice and then jumped up; first he went to the phone but when he was half-way through dialling Jeremy's number he put the phone down, ran to his bedroom, got dressed, and went down to his car outside the block of flats where he now lived.

Jeremy, eyes bleary, hair on end, came to open the front door of his flat in his pyjamas – he looked tired, but tired and pleased at the same time. 'Hullo, Donald,' he said, 'is it in the papers already? Your journalist friends must have had a hard night of it. Did it work properly?' Quick said nothing, simply handed the paper to Jeremy and went to sit down on the edge of Jeremy's bed. Jeremy opened the paper and read aloud, 'SABOTEURS BLOW RESERVOIR.' He looked at Quick and smiled; 'Pretty good, isn't it,' he said, 'headlines already.' Then he went back to reading the paper. 'Nightwatchman killed in explosion,' he read aloud. 'Oh, Christ, oh Christ,' Jeremy said and read again, 'Nightwatchman killed in explosion. Unknown saboteurs last night blew up the Helmet Reservoir near Belville. A native night-watchman has been found dead near the scene of the explosion. He is thought to have been killed by the blast.' Jeremy stopped reading; slowly he put the paper down and slowly came over to sit on the bed next to Quick. 'Oh my God, Donald, what happened? Do you know what happened?' he asked.

'How should I know? You should know, not me,' said Quick.

'Have you seen Hunter or the others?'

'No. I came straight here when I saw the headlines.'

'I don't understand,' said Jeremy. 'Roseman told us he was still in his hut just before the time. He couldn't have gone down there.'

'Why not?' said Quick. 'Why couldn't he?'

'Because Roseman was watching him all that time.'

'Couldn't he have gone down to investigate?'

'I was certain that he wouldn't; I was quite certain that he wouldn't. Why should he? He should have kept away, shouldn't he?'

'He didn't. Oh Christ, what are we going to do, Jeremy?'

'There's nothing that we can do.' Jeremy's face was set almost in a parody of hardness. 'Nothing, that's what we are going to do.'

'But this is murder now. You've killed someone, your bloody sabotage has killed someone.'

'It's not simply my sabotage, Donald.'

'But you should have made sure that the man didn't go down. Why didn't Roseman make sure?'

'How could he? We had to get away.'

The two young men sat quietly on the sofa, the newspaper on the floor in front of them; suddenly Quick got up, grabbed the paper, and started to the door.

'Where are you going?' asked Jeremy.

'To the office,' said Quick, 'to the office to see if I can find out anything more,' and he walked quickly out of the flat.

'Let me know, Donald,' shouted Jeremy. But Quick was out of earshot already for he did not reply.

At the meeting that night, which nobody dared to call by its usual name, Quick was able to add nothing to the reports which had appeared in the papers that morning and evening – the wall had gone, so had much of the pumping house, and the watchman had been found a few yards from the pumping house. He must have had his back to the second explosion, said one report, for he had extensive injuries to his back and to the back of his skull. No report seemed to state exactly what had happened to him; but all the group at their meeting realized that he must have heard the first explosion, must have come running down to see what had happened and, standing near the pumping house to watch the water roaring through the breached wall, must have taken the full force of the second explosion. The reports made it clear that there had been two explosions, for local residents had heard both clearly. Some said that thirty seconds separated them, some said fifteen minutes – but all said that there were two, the second sounding louder than the first; and Hunter explained in answer to Devis's question that the first must have been partly muffled.

The police said, as usual, that they hoped to make arrests shortly – a squad of Security policemen had spent the day there, said one evening newspaper, collecting evidence of the sabotage. There was no chance, said all the reports, that it had been an accident; the breach in the wall was clear evidence of foul play. The nightwatchman was not named, nor was there any mention of the woman Raymond Roseman had heard in his hut; she must have gone away, the group supposed, when the nightwatchman went down to investigate the first explosion.

That was all; and there was little said at the meeting. Stevens, speaking as chairman, said how sorry they all felt that this had happened but that it was entirely an accident which no one could have prevented or predicted. Roseman seemed too buried in his misery to point out that he had predicted this and no one took any notice when Quick shook his head at what Stevens said; but Quick did not say anything; and a little while afterwards the meeting ended.

6

What made Hunter begin to plan his escape was not the death of the nightwatchman. He had believed from the moment he was recruited that the idea of violence to installations without violence to people drew a distinction that practice would confound; and it did not particularly worry him that it was an African who had been killed – he was sorry for the man, as he would be sorry for any innocent victim, but he believed that, if his death had been necessary to the success of the sabotage, then it was justifiable. He had joined the organization despite the idea, not because of it; he had wanted to do something positive to change the country he had taken for his own and, whatever the limitations of the organization, it was at least fully committed to change.

No, what made him begin to plan for the end of the organization was his realization that he could not much longer go on relying on amateurs; up to the sabotage of the Helmet Reservoir he had thought that he might be able to get Jeremy to accept as necessary his code of professionalism – he had assumed that the others were not likely to accept his ideas, but Jeremy had seemed ripe for them. Certainly, in conversation he had responded to them; he had responded to the idea that a man might serve some power outside himself, he had seemed ready to accept that, in a revolutionary situation, the end justified the means. How often he had said to Jeremy that what they really needed was this kind of commitment, the sort of commitment that started by being voluntary and ended by being compelled; and Jeremy, though he often sneered at the idea, had seemed to be getting the same kind of discipline into his actions. Then it had all come tumbling down; not in a big way, but in the two little incidents that seemed to have passed almost unnoticed during the action at the reservoir. First, there had been Jeremy's disobedience of his instructions to crawl out along the wall; then there had been Jeremy's attempt to make them stop to listen for the explosions. As if that could have made any difference, thought Hunter; why, it had been pure vanity. The man was stuffed with vanity like a strawman was stuffed with straw. And you could not take it away because it was everything he was. He served only what was inside him, he served nothing else, nothing outside his own self.

He had tried so hard to make Jeremy see that; he had talked to him again and again, hoping to burst the balloon of egocentricity. 'The most marvellous thing about being in the army,' he had once told Jeremy, 'is the feeling you have of serving something outside yourself, the feeling that you don't belong to yourself only any more.'

'Like being a robot,' Jeremy replied.

'No, not like that at all. When you're leading a company or even a platoon you can't be a robot, your job is to be thoroughly alive both to yourself and to your men; but even when you are actually giving your own commands, you have this feeling of being outside yourself, of belonging to some greater power than your own senses and your own mind.'

'Even when you don't believe in what you are doing?' asked Jeremy, half-sneeringly, but only half, because he seemed to want to believe in the possibility of belonging to outside himself.

'Even then,' said Hunter. 'Even when you are doing something that you know you'll feel afterwards was morally wrong, something like destroying a village for strategic reasons, something like shooting badly wounded prisoners. . . .'

'Have you done that?' asked Jeremy; he looked sick at the thought.

'Yes,' said Hunter. 'Most professional soldiers have. Oh, good heavens, Jeremy, they would probably have died anyway.'

'It doesn't make it any better, does it?'

'No, of course not. I'm not saying that it is a good thing to do, I'm saying that you can do it when you have to.'

'I don't think I could do it.'

'You could, you know. Look, suppose we were doing something and it went badly wrong and I was chewed up in a blast, say, blinded and not able to walk. Wouldn't you shoot me then?'

'We don't carry guns.'

'We should, you know – and we should use them, if necessary.'

'I accept that,' said Jeremy. 'I accept that necessity in some situations; but. . . .'

'But not in this situation?' Hunter was pressing Jeremy hard.

'Yes, though I have some reservations still, even here.'

'And I have none. We must be prepared to kill – or, for that matter, to die.'

Jeremy laughed. 'I don't want to die, even if it's necessary,' he said.

Hunter was still completely serious: 'One day you may find it necessary to die,' he said; and because he was never afraid of saying what was simple and without intellectual sophistication, Hunter really believed this. The *naïveté* was always there; in a way, the *naïveté* was the intelligence; it was the ability not to divest logic of all emotion but to feel simplicity as being as real as sophistication. He was almost a tribesman, Jeremy thought, come from the interior with certain skills but no gods; now he was prepared to put his skills completely at the disposal of the tribe in return for a share of their gods. Yet he was not a fool; and he was not simply a professional soldier who worked for the best master; he did believe in things outside him, he did believe that he served some higher power than himself.

Jeremy believed Hunter; and he believed in him; and he tried to find the same power outside him – but he was equally a believer in Quick's kind of reality, the reality of unbelief, the reality of the continual question, the reality of the searcher. He could not believe, as Hunter did, that the answer lay outside him.

Of course, it was not enough for Hunter to plan his escape; there were other things to be done as well. He thought seriously about making his own approach to one of the African nationalist organizations; but he knew from Jeremy how little success there had been in the initial attempt to place the organization at the service of the African nationalists – and he suspected that any attempt he made from inside the country would get him nowhere. No, that was not the answer, he was sure; but there were other opponents of the present system and they might be able to help him find the kind of activity that he believed must be the next stage in creating a revolution. From them he would be able, at the least, to get the introductions to the African nationalist movements which he would need if he was to go any further.

Hunter did not abandon the organization; there were still things which he believed it could do and, anyway, in that situation, he believed that any form of opposition which could be kept alive had to be kept alive. The organization still deserved his care and attention; but there were other things to be done now.

Soon after Hunter began to plan his escape, Quick tried to resign from the organization.

At the start of the next meeting, which Quick himself organized, he said, 'Before we start, Ian, I want to say something. May I?' Stevens, who had some idea of what was coming, nodded and Quick went on, 'All of you know that I am meant to be a pacifist and that I agreed to join the organization only on condition that its activities did not extend to people. . . .'

'They weren't meant to,' interrupted Roseman. But Quick took no notice of him and went on again, 'It may have seemed strange that I as a pacifist should want to join a sabotage organization but I thought that I could reconcile the two things. When the nightwatchman was killed I had to think again – and I realized that I had been wrong to join you. Now I ask to leave. I want to resign.'

Roseman said bitterly, 'None of us wanted the nightwatchman to be killed.'

'I know,' said Quick. 'That's why I said carefully that it wasn't the death of the nightwatchman that made me want to resign – but it did force me to think again about my decision to join and I decided that had been wrong.'

Roseman did not seem to be listening properly, for he said, as if it were an answer, 'I feel myself in some way especially responsible for his death; I should have argued harder for his protection, I should have stayed longer.'

Stevens answered before anyone else could; he could see

Roseman's distress, a distress that Quick's intended resignation was making deeper. 'Raymond, if anyone is responsible, which I doubt, we share the responsibility equally – all of us, even me, even Quick.'

'I know,' said Quick. 'I know; but I can't take any more of that responsibility.'

'You have taken the responsibility already,' said Roseman.

'I know that,' said Quick. 'That's why I want to resign. You must let me resign. It's got nothing to do with the night-watchman; I made a mistake in the first place.'

Suddenly Stevens became the formal chairman again. 'Well, gentlemen,' he said, 'You've heard what Quick asks; are you willing that he should resign?'

For several moments there was silence. Then Devis said, 'No.'

'What?' said Quick.

'No,' said Devis.

'I agree,' said Hunter.

'But why?' said Quick. He laughed, not as a man might who has found the world funny but as a man would who had found that his path over the mountains had been rushed away in a landslide. 'Surely you can't force me to stay if I don't want to? Surely you agree that I should be allowed to resign from the organization, now, if I want to?' Quick was looking at Jeremy who would not look back at him. 'Jeremy?' said Quick but still Jeremy did not look at him. 'Jeremy, did you hear me?'

'Yes, I heard,' said Jeremy and sat quietly, still not looking at Quick. Then he looked up at Stevens and said, to Stevens and not to Quick, 'Yes, Mr Chairman, I agree with Devis and Hunter that Quick should not be allowed to resign.' He still did not look at Quick.

'Good heavens, this is ludicrous,' burst out Quick. 'I only asked as a formality. Look, I'm not just asking to resign, I'm demanding to resign.'

'My answer is still no,' said Hunter. He was smiling.

'And mine,' said Devis.

'And you, Jeremy?' asked Quick. 'Are you going to try to force me to stay in? And you, Raymond? And you, Stevens?'

'This is not really my decision,' said Stevens. 'It must be a group decision. After all, I am hardly involved in the group any more.' Everyone looked at him and so he corrected himself; 'I mean, I am not actively involved – I am only part of the planning side now.'

'If that's what you meant . . .' said Devis. He, like Roseman and Quick, did not realize the full implication of what Stevens had said.

'Yes, of course; it was simply a slip of my tongue,' said Stevens. Hunter was looking hard at him. He went on quickly, 'Hunter and Devis seem to agree about Quick's resignation. What about you, Raymond?'

'I agree with the others – Donald should not be allowed to resign.'

'Why?' said Quick. 'Why, I ask you?'

'Because this isn't something you resign from – if you come in, you stay in.'

'Even if I disagree violently with your decisions?'

'Yes,' said Roseman. 'Once in, you stay in – you can't opt out.'

'Bloody hell I can't,' said Quick. 'Jeremy, do you really think you can try to force me to stay in?'

'I'm not sure that we can force you,' said Jeremy, looking at Quick for the first time since the meeting had started. 'But I am sure that we can still consider you to be a member. Even if you were to refuse to do anything at all, we could still keep you in.'

'Why?' said Quick. 'Why? If I refuse to do anything.'

'Because we can't have ex-members wandering about,' said Devis.

'If you are implying that I intend to inform on you, you can get stuffed – I am not a traitor, I just want to get out of this organization.'

'If you get out, you are a traitor,' said Jeremy quietly.

'Nonsense,' said Quick. 'Anyway, it doesn't matter – I intend to resign. There is nothing anyone can do to stop me. Suppose I got up now and just walked out, who would stop me?' He got to his feet and started for the door.

As Quick put his hand on the door handle and started to open it, Devis caught him; grabbed him by the arm, swung him round, and then caught his jacket front with both hands, pulling him away from the door. Quick, taken by surprise, let Devis pull him back from the door before he tried to free himself from Devis's grip. When he could not, he pulled himself back as far as he could from Devis, and, almost coldly, hit Devis right-handed in the face, striking him on the side of his nose and top lip. Devis, trying to block the punch, let go with one hand and Quick brought his left hand down on Devis's wrist, forcing him to let go completely. Devis was holding his bleeding mouth with both hands but Quick did not attempt to move to the door now; instead he stepped forward and, again right-handed, hit Devis hard under the heart. As Devis doubled forward, Quick started to bring his knee up to take Devis in the face once again; but before his knee connected, Hunter had managed to get round from the far side of the room and he shoved Quick hard so that his knee-kick only glanced Devis's shoulder. Off-balance, Quick staggered against the wall and half-fell and, before he could recover himself, Hunter was behind him and had his arms locked tight to his sides. Roseman was there too by that time and he helped Hunter control Quick, who was struggling to get free; and Stevens was there to prevent Devis, now ready to fight again, from coming forward to attack Quick.

The one person who had not moved was Jeremy; he sat in his chair, watching Hunter and Roseman holding Quick, and Stevens trying to make Devis let him look at his cut mouth, which was now bleeding badly. Jeremy could see the blood coming through Devis's fingers. He waited until Hunter and Roseman seemed to have Quick firmly held and then said, with all the bitterness which he could muster, 'That is the most dramatic resignation I have ever seen. For God's sake, Quick and the rest of you, sit down and stop behaving like children.' It was the first word that had been said since Quick started to move for the door, for, from the moment Devis had grabbed him, everyone except Jeremy had been too concerned with his own anger and his own desire to want to speak, even to swear. Hunter and Roseman now let Quick go; they stood with him for a moment to see that he was not going to start fighting again and then left him. Quick looked at the door for a moment; he seemed to be making up his mind whether he would go out of it but then he too went to sit down. Only Devis and Stevens were not sitting now and then Devis sat down while Stevens went off to get a wet towel to try to stop the bleeding.

While he was gone no one talked; and when he came back, it was only he who talked to Devis, as he mopped away at the split mouth – the others sat quiet, letting the rage die away. At last, the bleeding seemed to have stopped and Stevens too went to sit down, throwing the towel into a corner of the room.

Devis turned to Quick and tried to smile. 'I thought you were a pacifist,' he said out of the uninjured corner of his mouth.

'I used to be quite a good boxer,' said Quick. 'I'm sorry, I hope the mouth isn't too bad. I caught it quite a crack.'

'Christ,' said Roseman. 'If you learnt that knee-kick trick in the boxing ring, I'm glad I wasn't at school with you.'

'No,' said Quick, 'I learnt that somewhere else.'

'It's a good thing it didn't connect,' said Hunter. 'I only just managed to push you in time.'

'Yes,' said Quick. He could feel pleasure in one part of him and disgust in another – pleasure that he had put Devis down so fast, disgust that he felt pleasure.

'You sound as if you're discussing some boxing match you've seen,' said Stevens. He sounded almost amused.

'Yes,' said Jeremy. 'Yes and it is bloody disgusting – Quick is disgusting, Devis is disgusting, all of you are disgusting. Can't you see what is happening? Can't you? You are letting happen to you what you should not – you are letting what we have to do corrupt you. You are out of control, all of you.' He turned to Quick and went on, raging but holding his rage so that he too would not want to fight, 'You and your pacifism, Quick. I know all about it; but you don't do it because you believe in it but because you are afraid of it. You try to cut it out of you, don't you? And all the time it sits there and when you get a chance, like just now, you revel in it; you enjoyed that, didn't you? It was good to feel Devis go down, wasn't it? It was a marvellously timed piece of hitting; and you are really quite proud of it, aren't you? And perhaps you feel a little guilty now, do you? And one emotion sits on top of the other, like a turkey on a barn? Well, I think it disgusting, I think you're disgusting.'

'In fairness to Donald,' said Devis, 'I did go for him first, Jeremy.'

'Ah, the sporting instinct,' said Jeremy. 'You make me sick too, Arthur – you'd always shake hands with the man who beat you, wouldn't you? That way it makes it all right, doesn't it? Three cheers for the winner, three cheers for the loser, three cheers for the referees; "a jolly good match, what – pity about old Arthur's mouth; still a couple of stitches will see it right. Good to see such a hard match again",' all this in the fruity voice of a sportsman, 'I tell you, it makes me sick, the whole bloody thing is enough to make me sick.'

'Just what is the point of the tirade, Jeremy?' asked Stevens. 'Or do you want to go on now?'

'I just wanted to tell you what I thought,' said Jeremy. He turned to Quick, 'Well, Donald, when are you resigning?'

'I don't think that I am resigning after all,' said Quick quietly.

' "Oh, damn fine show, old chap",' said Jeremy in the fruity voice again. ' "The gallant winner then gave half his purse to the loser".'

Quick was up again; half-crouching, he screamed at Jeremy, 'Shut up, you bastard, before I do you too.'

'Sit down, Donald,' said Roseman. 'Jeremy, stop being a bloody fool.'

'Oh, I'm behaving badly now, am I?' said Jeremy. 'Roseman the Fearless is telling me to be quiet, is he? Roseman the Fearless stopped one fight, admittedly with the help of Hunter, and now he wants to prevent another.'

Roseman said nothing; he was much the biggest man in the room and now he was having to hold himself in his chair. If Jeremy had said another word to him, he would have been out of the chair. But Jeremy knew too well what he was doing, for he turned now to Devis and said, in a very polite voice, 'I must congratulate you, Mr Devis, on having persuaded Mr Quick to withdraw his resignation. I do hope that your lip is not too badly injured.'

But now Hunter stepped in; Stevens, he could see, was out of control of the situation. 'Jeremy,' said Hunter. 'I think that you had better stop whatever it is you are trying to do.' Jeremy turned now to Hunter and the others could see that he was about to start on him too; but Hunter prevented him by saying, 'Don't you start on me, Jeremy. I have a good idea what you would say and I don't think that you had better.' The menace in his voice was such that even Jeremy could not go on; still, he had done most of what he had intended to do, he had brought the group together again and he was certain that he could now bring himself back in again. He smiled at Hunter; 'All right,' he said, 'I have finished.'

Now Stevens tried to take control back into his own hands – coldly he said to Jeremy, 'Though you have finished, hadn't you better say what on earth you were going on about?'

Jeremy could not help himself when he started to reply; 'Oh, yes, Mr Chairman,' he said, allowing all the scorn he could muster to dwell on the words – he was telling Stevens that he was a failure, that the group was now beyond his control; he was, if you like, paying Stevens back for having seemed to say earlier that he was not really involved in the group.

Stevens knew just what Jeremy meant and started to speak, but Hunter again interrupted the conversation to say, 'Jeremy, I told you to shut up. Now will you get on with what you have to say without being rude to anyone?' Jeremy chose to obey Hunter; it was a choice, he was not being bullied into behaving himself, he was choosing – he was, at that moment, completely in control of his mind.

'All right,' he said. 'I was simply trying to show you all what was happening to you – and surely you can see? You were, you are, on the point of disintegration. Quick said simply what you were all waiting for, a chance to get at someone else, someone who had to be in the group because you could not talk to anyone outside it. I bet you that Roseman had been thinking of resigning; haven't you, Raymond?'

'Yes,' said Roseman. 'I have. I decided not to; but I thought about it.'

'I bet you, too, that all of you have thought about whether there was any point in the organization going on, after what happened last time.' Jeremy looked around the room; both Stevens and Devis nodded – they had thought for a time that the best thing that could be done was to call the group off, to pack the whole thing in. Only Hunter did not nod; he sat and watched Jeremy very carefully.

'All right,' Jeremy went on. 'And because you had been thinking that perhaps you should pack up the group, you all hoped that someone else would give you the chance – Quick did and that was why there was a fight. That was why I attacked all of you – I had to make you see.'

Still no one spoke; Jeremy paused to see if anyone wanted to interrupt and then he went on; 'Look, this was bound to happen. There was bound to be a stage when the group started to fall apart. That's why you can't resign, Donald; there's no other reason. If you go, everyone will start to go. Don't you see, Donald? It doesn't matter really what you actually do – you can do nothing but you have to remain a member of the group if anyone is going to remain. Don't you see, all of you?' Jeremy felt so sure of what he was saying that it seemed to him that the others must see; he looked at Hunter – this was, he knew, Hunter's voice speaking through him but he could not be sure that even Hunter would understand. 'Isn't it true, Hunter?' he asked.

'Of course,' said Hunter – it was true and he recognized what Jeremy was trying to do. Jeremy did believe in the organization; what Hunter was not sure of was whether Jeremy believed in the organization more than he believed in himself – and you could not take risks about something like that.

'Isn't it true, the rest of you?' asked Jeremy. Stevens and Devis nodded but both Quick and Roseman made no sign even that they had heard. They have to understand, thought Jeremy, they have to. He began again: 'Look, if one person can go because he is unhappy about something that has happened, then you have to start working on the basis of what holds us together – and that ...' he searched for the right phrase – how could he make Quick in particular see? 'lowest common denominator,' he said – that's the right image for Quick, he thought – 'has got nothing to do with action, it's only an idea. Yet you have to see that ideas aren't enough any more, it's got to be what you do, even if someone like Donald doesn't like it. Do you see what I mean?'

For a moment or two he was afraid that Roseman and Quick had not seen; he looked at Quick – it was on him that what happened now depended. If he was right, and he was sure that he was right, Quick had to say that he accepted what had been said; and now Quick said something that was not everything that Jeremy had wanted but that was enough. 'Yes, Jeremy, I don't entirely accept all that you say, but I won't resign,' he said and now Jeremy knew that he had won.

In a way he had won, for the group stayed together to the end. But in another way the disintegration had started well before that; it had started, Quick decided afterwards, not because of anything that had happened in the group itself, it had started with other betrayals and those betrayals too had started a long way before then, had started perhaps before any person in the group was born, had started three hundred years before, when the first white man came to South Africa, had started even before that. There was nothing that any person could do about that; it happened because the gods had so determined it – and if you do not believe in the gods, and if you believe, as Jeremy believed, in the responsibility each man has to himself, you will have to choose your own place to start the series. When you have counted backwards, when you can say, here it started, or here, or here, count forwards again and see whether you have the same series at the end. If you have the same, perhaps you are another Jeremy; and then you had better start working out your answer to the next problem.

The group did nothing more as a group; Quick, though he stayed a member, was so afraid of letting the darkness flood to his head again that he could do almost nothing; Roseman was so afraid of making another mistake like the one he had made, or thought he had made, that he became almost useless; and Stevens had, as he said, never been an activist. Hunter, Jeremy, and Devis, more as a joke than with serious intent, blew up a statue of Onze Jan Hofmeyr, father of the man who had once been the hope of South African liberalism – they simply mined the legs of the horse on which Onze Jan sat and the horse and Jan toppled over into the street. Quick was momentarily useful here; he managed to get his newspaper to suggest that this was really a prank by the students of the Afrikaans University – and the group hoped that if the police were beginning to know too much they might be put off the trail. Then Hunter and Jeremy, without the aid or even the knowledge of the rest of the group, blew up three telephone kiosks in the suburbs; it was, they knew, a futile gesture but there seemed little else left. By the time that the rest of the group realized that they were responsible for these petty operations, it was already clear that the group, despite all efforts, was more or less pointless; they did not disband, there was no reason to do that – each member simply went on as he had done before the advent of the group and only Hunter seemed to want to find other people with whom to work; for Jeremy at least, if no one else in the group, knew that Hunter was beginning to see more and more of the few white communists in Cape Town who had not joined the exodus to London and a free society. But Jeremy knew too that Hunter seemed to have found a more or less permanent girl, one apparently without political connections, a girl called Patricia Richmond; so he did not worry much about what he thought were Hunter's deviations, because the one seemed to cancel the other.

7

All their friends thought that Mary Dobling suited Quick – certainly she was attractive, not too tall, slim but with such full breasts that, as a young girl, she had learned to stoop slightly to try to conceal them, and that not-quite blonde hair which, cut short, looks both natural and feminine. She had never lost the slight stoop; but now she had such an awareness of her body that it made the stoop seem both unplanned and provocative, as if concealment equalled display. Yet, unlike most sexually aware women, she had, Quick found, very little control over her own sexuality; she became, when she was excited, almost animal.

But though Quick enjoyed her sensuality, though he was pleased to be seen with such an attractive girl, though he enjoyed being with her, he did not think that he loved her – he found her, for someone reading for a post-graduate degree in English, amazingly inarticulate and to someone like Quick this was tiresome. She was intelligent, she was grown-up, she was attractive, but she could not talk; it seemed to him that her sensuality was so strong that words were useless to her.

'How on earth can you get a degree in words if you can't use them?' he would tease her.

'I can use them,' she would say. 'I write perfectly well, I'm just no good at saying things.'

'Then why don't you write letters to me?'

'Because I couldn't say anything except "I am well", "How are you?" and "When are you going to take me to bed again?", she would answer and Quick would be so anxious to answer her last question that he would forget that she could never talk to him. But later, the doubt would return – how could Mary, he would think, know anything when she couldn't say anything. No, he did not love her, he thought, however good it was to make love to her – and, because he did not love her, he decided that she could not love him either. Still, said their friends, they went well together and they'd probably end up getting married; it was not simply a student affair, it was much more passionate and involved than that, they said.

But when Jeremy started taking Sheilagh Owen out, none of their friends thought it would work; for one thing, Jeremy was known to distrust physical beauty and Sheilagh was, if not beautiful, nearly so. For another, Jeremy was known to be puritan about sex; and, anyway, they said, there was that man-eating mother of his. For another, Jeremy himself said, and everyone agreed, that he really did not have time for serious love affairs. Yet his affair with Sheilagh lasted; she was not the only girl he was seen with but she was with him more often than any other – and particularly after Jeremy gave up the cottage, he and Sheilagh came as near to living together, said their friends, as they could without actually sharing the same house. Nobody supposed that Jeremy was in love with her, not at any rate in the usual sense; but he was fond of her and she seemed content with that, if only because she had to be. He really did not have time to love anyone full-time; he was always too busy with other work. They wouldn't marry, said their friends, but they seemed to have worked out some happiness between them, for Sheilagh seemed to worship Jeremy and Jeremy liked Sheilagh.

The two girls, their friends often said, looked almost like sisters; they had the same kind of slim full-breasted bodies and not-quite-blond hair and clear, wide-set eyes, and they dressed alike – they were too attractive to want to look like dowdy political women but they did not want, either, to seem too clothes-conscious. But in most ways their minds worked very differently. Sheilagh came from as near a working-class home as it was possible for a white South African to have; her parents were good solid working people who lived in Retreat. You would have expected, said her friends, that she would have moved away from them when she got her scholarship and went to university – but though she lived, first, in a university residence and, then, from about the same time as Quick left the cottage, in a room of her own, she seemed close to her parents still – her father, a printing-house manager, gave her enough extra money for her to be able to run a small car and the less kind of her friends said that was why she still visited her parents. She was articulate as Mary was silent, tough, as hard-working as her father, though she was, by training as a doctor, moving out of her class; she sailed through her medical exams and had time to spare for politics; she became a liberal on her own, for her home was just like any other white South African one, ignorant, smug, and prejudiced – and Quick and Jeremy assumed that she had become a liberal just because she was intelligent, for none of their circle thought that it was possible to be both intelligent and conservative, even intelligent and racialist, at the same time. But her liberalism was not simply a matter of intelligence – she had been so determined to succeed at the university that she almost automatically caught the mood of the place, which was at that time more or less liberal; and that was nothing remarkable – it was the way most university liberals were formed.

It was not that she did not think for herself, it was simply that she was dependent on her surroundings in a way that made her seem, sometimes, almost stupid. Once she had been caught by the mood of an idea, she would work out the idea for herself stage by stage and then believe that she had come to the idea independently. But it was not true; she caught the feeling from her surroundings, from her friends, and then she worked out the ideas for herself – she could analyse but she could not create.

Mary was, like Quick, a liberal almost by birth. She was the second daughter of an Anglican clergyman from the Transvaal and, when Quick teased her for being so unlike the usual clergyman's daughter, she used to reply, seriously, that she was sure that her father understood her behaviour as well as anyone; her sister, she said, had been just the same. 'I'm sure,' she went on, 'that she used to sleep with the boys she brought home to stay, even while she was at school – and I'm sure that Daddy knew and wasn't shocked.'

'Amazing kind of clergyman,' Quick would say.

'Yes,' Mary replied. 'Yes, he is but he is still a clergyman,' and Quick, who loved his own father, would laugh at her, not at all jeeringly, because he knew that she loved her father and he teased her only because he thought she was right to love him.

Once Quick had left the cottage, it seemed that not only did Jeremy and Sheilagh become closer but that it was easier for the four of them, Jeremy and Sheilagh, he and Mary, to be friends. It seemed to him that the tension between Mary and Jeremy, the tension that he thought was caused by Jeremy's dislike of her sensuality, had disappeared; he seems almost to like Mary now, thought Quick – and that in its turn made it easier for him to be friends with Jeremy, because he seemed more natural now, much less the thorny puritan. Moreover, both Jeremy and Quick had decided that they did not love their girls and they used, when they were on their own, to say so to each other; and this too seemed to bring them closer together again, almost as close, thought Quick, as we used to be when I moved in to share the cottage with him.

Afterwards, when the series was complete, when the numbers were all there to be played with, Quick often wondered why he had not seen the truth before he was told it – it was as though, for more than a year, he had lain asleep in a slowly burning house and that, by the time he had woken up to the smell of smoke and the crash of rafters, there was nothing left to do but to get out of the house. Could he have woken up before, he would wonder. What would he have done if he had woken up, if he had been in time to prevent the fire from taking hold? Would he still have walked out, taking no chances, or would he have stayed inside to fight it with whatever means he could have found? But even if you left those numbers out of the series, it might have been possible, he knew, to put them together into something of the same order, because he would have not known then more than one or two or three; the difficult numbers he could never have worked out, for you just had to wait for them, you just had to wait until they were dropped down from the celestial computer on to your table. The gods were, for Quick, poor mathematicians; they set their problems without giving you enough information to allow you to find any kind of probable answer until everything had gone through their own machine and you were presented with an answer.

8

When Quick was released from detention, one hundred and twenty-three days after his arrest, it was generally known that Jeremy had talked. What Quick was able to add to the rumours was the definite information that Jeremy had talked, had broken as Quick called it, in less than two days – for, by the end of his third day in detention, Sergeant Viljoen had questioned Quick using as a basis for his questions a typed document that Quick had gradually realized was Jeremy's confession. Though the sergeant was careful not to show it fully to Quick, the questions he asked were not really questions needing answers; rather, they were statements of fact which he wanted confirmed. 'Is it so, Mr Quick, that on the night of 14 May the Helmet Reservoir at Belville was destroyed by four of your people?' he would ask.

At first Quick lied. 'They were not "my people", Sergeant, and although I heard about it at the newspaper office and read it in the papers, I know nothing else about it.' So the sergeant chalked on the floor a little square, big enough for Quick's feet only, and told him to stand in it. He repeated the question and, when Quick did not reply, went away, leaving Quick standing in the square. Quick was not sure how long the sergeant stayed away; there was a clock on the wall but he forgot to look at it when the sergeant left and, by the time he did look, he was not sure how long he had been standing already. When the sergeant came back, he repeated the question. Quick answered again that he knew only what he had read in newspapers. The sergeant repeated the question, this time with embellishments: 'Let us be more specific, Mr Quick. Which one of your people was it who fixed a prepared explosive charge to the pumping house at the Helmet Reservoir, that charge which killed the native nightwatchman?' Quick said nothing. The sergeant waited quarter of an hour, then repeated the question. After about two hours, he went away and another Security policeman came in and asked the same question, at long intervals, but still getting no reply. Three hours later the sergeant reappeared. This time he prefaced the question by saying, 'You are being very stupid, Mr Quick. Which one of your people was it . . .' and so on.

After eight hours' standing Quick fainted. He was brought to by a policeman's throwing a glass of water in his face. The sergeant and a constable helped him from the floor and stood him in the square again. This time he lasted only an hour and the next only ten minutes. When it became clear that Quick could no longer stand unaided, the sergeant rubbed out one square and chalked another next to the wall. With the wall to support him Quick found it easier to stand – he lasted four hours like that. The sergeant then let him sit down for ten minutes, gave him a cup of tea and a sandwich which he said his wife had made, and then stood him next to the wall again.

After thirty-six hours they carried him back to his cell and left him for a week. Twice a day he would be allowed half an hour's exercise in the yard; he would be brought food from the police kitchen twice a day and once every two or three days he was given parcels of fruit, sweets, and cigarettes from his family and clean clothes which Mary had brought for him. He used to search everything very carefully for messages that they might have tried to smuggle in but he did not find anything. Next time he was questioned, all the sergeant had to do was to draw the chalk square. Quick knew that the police knew all he had to tell them and once he had answered the first question there seemed no point in not answering the rest. But he refused to make the full statement which the sergeant wanted from him. They did not bother to stand him in the square this time; they took him back to his cell, left him there, and removed his privileges of exercise and parcels from the outside. After four days Quick asked to see the sergeant again and told him that he would make a full statement.

After the statement was made, typed, and signed, Quick was transferred from Woodstock to Sea Point police cells. He was allowed his privileges again and was even allowed the books and writing materials which his father brought to the police station for him. But he did not see the Security police again for more than four weeks; the only people he saw were the ordinary policemen who came to let him out for his exercise each day, who brought him the parcels from Mary and his father, who let in a coloured prisoner each day to clean his cell, and who stood in the doorway watching the coloured prisoner until he had finished.

Arthur Devis was more difficult. When he was first taken in for questioning, after five days in solitary detention, Sergeant Van der Post used the same technique that Quick had undergone; Arthur was told to stay standing in the chalked square and, soon afterwards, the sergeant went away, leaving Devis standing – but, alone, he didn't stand for long; he left the square and sat down in one of the two chairs in the room to wait for the sergeant's return. When he came back in, he was obviously amused to see Devis sitting in the chair. He stood in the door for a moment, then said, 'I thought you would do that, Mr Devis – you would not wait for me to come, would you? Well, stay there for the moment,' and he came to sit on the desk in front of Arthur. He looked at Arthur sitting in the chair, and, casually, put a foot on the arm of the straight-backed chair. 'Well, Mr Devis,' and suddenly he pushed the chair in which Arthur was sitting over backwards; there was nothing that Arthur could do, he tried frantically to get the chair back on a level, but he had to fall and he came down heavily, just managing to tip sideways as he hit the floor. He lay there for a moment, dazed; then he looked up at the sergeant who was now standing near him, still smiling. Devis started to try to get to his feet, saying as he did so, 'You bastard.' The sergeant kicked him hard in his left side and he fell again; he tried not to scream but could not help it. 'Now get back in that square,' said the sergeant; he was not angry, rather he sounded like a schoolmaster explaining something to a stupid pupil. Arthur, now crouched on the floor, could only just manage to stand, so the sergeant took him by the arm and held him up and, then, lightly, slapped his face, palm-stroke, and, then, harder, backhand. Arthur, still in pain from the kick in his kidneys, reacted like an animal; his hands came up and he tried to grab the sergeant's throat; afterwards, he remembered with surprise that he had not said anything, had not even sworn, had simply tried to kill the sergeant – and, ordinarily, he would have come close to succeeding, for the sergeant was not a big man. But the noise of the scuffles brought two constables through the door of the sergeant's office and Arthur was torn off and thrown in the corner while the constables helped the sergeant from the floor.

He was still smiling, a tight little smile as a man might have who looked at an obscene photograph, though his throat was red where Arthur had held him. He and the constables walked over to the corner where Devis lay, watching them. Suddenly, Devis knew that he was smiling too; he was winning, he thought, he was winning. He still wasn't scared, he thought, he wasn't scared like he had been after they had arrested him, in some strange way he was winning. Seeing him smile, one of the constables drew back his foot to kick him again; but the sergeant, who saw the smile too, prevented the kick roughly, and ordered Devis to stand up. With the help of the wall he did so. 'Now stand in that square.' Devis did not move so almost gently the sergeant took his arm and led him to the square. The constables went over to the wall behind the desk and the sergeant sat in his chair again: 'Now you will answer some questions, Devis. I want to know the names of the Cape Town branch.' Arthur shook his head. The sergeant waited a full minute, then stood up. 'Come on,' he said to the constables. 'Let us leave him here to think,' and he ushered the constables out of his office before him and, as he paused at the door, Arthur left the square and went to sit down, this time in the sergeant's chair itself.

The sergeant smiled again and called down the corridor after the constables. 'Jannie, Hendrik, kom terug. He is still trying to create troubles.' They came back in and the three stood around the desk. Arthur could not resist the theatrical gesture, so stretched his legs out and said, 'Well, gentlemen, what can I do for you?' though he knew that it was ham acting and that his voice shook. The pause, the tight little smile, and then, 'I think that you are going to try to escape, Mr Devis. Will we help him to escape, Jannie? I think so. Bring him.'

So the constables pulled Arthur from the chair and walked him down the corridor to the head of the flight of stone stairs which led to the charge office below. The sergeant danced down the stairs and stood at the locked door below while the constables stood each side of Arthur at the top of the stairs. 'Turn him round,' called the sergeant, then, 'All right now,' and the constables pushed Arthur, not really very hard but so that, as he staggered back, trying to get a footing on the stairs, he had a vision of the whole world contained in the laughing faces of the constables; and then the walls staggered with him, his legs twisted, and he fell sideways down the stairs, rolling and sliding until the thud of the sergeant's boot in his groin as he reached the bottom of the stairs seemed almost welcome.

Next day, when the magistrate made his weekly visit to detainees as he was required to do by law, he did not even ask Arthur if he had any complaints; he called the commandant into the cell, pointed at Arthur who lay on a mattress in the far corner of the cell, and said, 'What happened to him?'

'He tried to escape, I'm afraid to say, sir,' the commandant replied, 'and he fought the constables – one of my men has a badly bruised throat too.' Arthur did not bother to say, You bloody liar, because he was still winning and he knew that he was winning; he had not said a word that could harm anyone.

But they broke him too in the end, though it took a long time and no more violence, for Sergeant Viljoen took over the questioning – and he apologized to Devis for his colleague's behaviour, doing as Arthur had known would be done, pretending to be the good man protecting the defenceless from the bad. The violence had, in a way, helped him; it gave him someone specific to hate and yet he was not fooled by apparent kindness. It took the police such a long time to break him that when, after ninety days in detention, they were forced by the law to release him and then arrest him again at the door of the police station, he still had not made the statement they wanted; not that it made much difference to anyone but Arthur, because by then they had statements from, of the Cape Town people alone, Jeremy, Quick, and Stevens – and they wanted Arthur to talk not because they needed it for evidence for the trial but as a sign that he had broken. After a time they got the statement; and they got too, for a while, an offer from him to turn state evidence – but he changed his mind and, anyway, the police did not want him, because they had Jeremy from the start and, from their point of view, he looked an even better witness.

In the end, you can break almost anybody if you keep him alone for long enough, because we are men only as much as we belong to other men – that became part of Quick's creed later, though it was a strange kind of creed which began, 'In the end, you can break almost anybody. . . .' Some are broken by violence, some are strengthened by it; but all are destroyed by being alone. Perhaps the simplest of us, the Robinson Crusoes, will survive longer than most, thought Quick – but perhaps he believed that only because he believed that he was not simple himself. Did the quickness of your breaking depend on your complexity as a person? Quick was never sure but he was sure that everyone would break in the end. You could not praise the exceptions, those who would rather die than face their own limited strength, those who escape being alone by peopling solitude with their own creations, angels and archfiends crowding a cell, or gibbering ghosts, or a society of mysterious friends. It seemed good to hold out for a long time, it seemed bad to talk too quickly. But, thought Quick, you could forgive, you had to forgive, anyone who simply told the police what he knew – what seemed unforgivable was that, though you broke because you were alone, you were prepared, when you came back to a more normal world, still to practise your solitude to the extent of betraying your friends so that you could save yourself. It was all right, thought Quick, to make a statement; merit could be achieved by not making it too soon; the step which made you a traitor was not that which told the police what they probably knew already, but that which turned you into a state witness when you were prepared to barter your friends for your freedom. He knew that Arthur had done right and that Jeremy had done wrong; and even if he could not explain why, he knew that he did not fit his own scale of right and wrong. He had to fit in somewhere, he thought; somewhere between being a traitor and being a hero. Jeremy was the traitor; Arthur was near to being a hero.

Stevens was a kind of hero too. It took the police seventy days to get him to answer one question; when he was first detained, he gave his name, address, and next-of-kin, and then for seventy days did not say another word, to the magistrate, to the ordinary policemen, to the men who came to clean his cell, to the embezzler who was for one night locked up in the cell next to him, to the other prisoners who shouted from nearby cells. When, after seventy days, they had tried everything to make him speak, and he had still not said a word, not even 'no', they brought to him in his cell a pile of typed documents; on the top was Jeremy's detailed confession, and under it were the copies of the statements by Quick, by the other national organizer, and by seven of the other people who had been arrested in other regions of the country. Stevens read them through, one after the other and, when he had finished, he went to stand at the cell door until the Security police came back. When they came, they asked him, 'Have you read the documents, Mr Stevens?' He hesitated for a moment, swallowed, cleared his throat, and then said, 'Yes.' It came out very loudly and the policemen smiled. They asked him then whether he was prepared to make a statement but he refused and went on refusing for a long time; in the end, the police had to be content with a short statement which said only that he had read the statements made by other detainees about sabotage and that he was prepared to say that all the details which concerned him were correct. All he added to this was that he intended to plead guilty at his trial; and then he stopped talking again until they had charged him.

Sheilagh Owen was neither heroine nor traitor; and nobody blamed her. When she was arrested, half an hour after the police had let her leave Jeremy's flat, she was trying to load explosives into the boot of her car from the garage in Mowbray where they were stored. They took her straight to Jeremy's cell, unlocked the door, and pushed her in; and they stood in the doorway and laughed as she tried to comfort him.

'Why don't you tell her to get undressed and into bed, Mr Jeremy?' said a constable.

'She'd like that, we interrupted you last time,' said another.

'Come on man, get her jersey off.'

'Christ, man, if I had half the chances you've had, I wouldn't be sitting there – hell, you university students really know what to do in your spare time.'

'Come on man, don't mind us. Go ahead, we're only watching.'

Jeremy did not move, he sat on the mattress on the floor, his head turned to the wall, an arm thrown up to protect himself – and Sheilagh kneeled near him, a hand on his back, trying to talk to him, trying to ignore the jeering of the policemen. And when she could stand it no longer, when she turned to scream at them, 'Go away, damn you, you've done all you need to, go away,' they mocked her and pretended for a moment to go away, closing the cell door as if they would leave them there alone; and then they came in again and now they pretended to be shocked and said, 'We really can't have this – man, here's a prisoner brought a woman in here,' and 'Really, it is disgusting – you'd think they got enough without having to do that kind of thing here,' and 'You're no better than a whore, my girl'; even then Jeremy did not move.

So they took her away; and next morning they brought to see Jeremy Sheilagh's parents, her good solid parents, her good solid liberal-hating God-fearing parents, who seemed almost as shocked that their daughter had been found in bed with a man as they were that the police had said that the man was a saboteur. The police left them there for only ten minutes; and both cursed Jeremy and Mrs Owen had wept and Mr Owen had threatened and Jeremy had said nothing except, 'Don't blame me,' and then, 'I'm sorry.' Immediately after they took Sheilagh's parents away, they brought into Jeremy not his mother, who stood in the charge office below demanding to see her son, but his father; and he, beautiful weak old man, had wept and prayed and besought his son to confess, to tell him all that he knew, to tell the police all that he knew, to make good the wrong which he had done. Mrs Jeremy was not allowed to see him at all, even after he had made his statement, a day and a half later.

Sheilagh at first refused to talk to the police; she asked only to see Jeremy, nothing else; and even when her father shook her until she could not stand, she refused to say anything except, 'Let me see Jeremy.' So, when Jeremy had made his statement, the police took her back to him and he told her that, since he had said all he could, she might as well too. When she stood in his cell, listening to him, not explaining why, for he never did that, but simply telling her to follow his example, it seemed to her almost that he did not recognize her; and when, as the police took her away, she said to him, 'I love you, Jeremy,' not caring that the police heard, he only shook his head as if to say, Love doesn't come into this.

So she made her statement; and she was, two weeks later, released from detention into the custody of her parents, who promised that they would keep her away from the university and her university friends; and not so much because of her parents but because she herself did not want to see anyone, she kept her parents' promise for them, refusing to talk to the press, refusing to see her friends, refusing to leave her parents' house even to go for a walk.

Roseman and Hunter got safely away, Roseman to Zambia and then to London, Hunter to Bechuanaland and then to one of the African states to the north. In fact, however, Hunter's name never came out publicly, though there was some gossip about a 'mysterious sixth member' and even, at a few parties, of his having been an *agent provocateur*. But, perhaps mainly because he was the one professional in a group of amateur saboteurs, the Security police chose to keep quiet about him and so no one knew much.

Patricia Richmond was questioned by the police after Jeremy's confession and again later when her car was discovered near the border – but since she had already told the police that she had lent her car to Hunter, not even the police could suggest that she had done it for a deliberate purpose. Various other of their friends were questioned and one or two even detained for a few hours; but with what Jeremy had told them, the police knew that they had all the Cape Town group except Hunter and Roseman;

and any other arrests they made were as much to intimidate as to investigate.

There was no secrecy about Roseman; his beach-front meetings with Stevens, his doubts about the operation at the Helmet Reservoir, and his escape, were all talked about at the trial; and, among some, there was admiring talk about his escaping so easily. Mrs Roseman left the country with her children before the trials started; the Security police were at the airport to watch her leave but they did not speak to her or to the children.

No one, not even Quick himself, was exactly sure why he was not charged; it seemed to be partly because he had not ever played an active part in sabotage, although Quick did not understand how the police managed to draw a line between handing out explosives to saboteurs and placing them yourself; it seemed to be partly that he had made an attempt to resign after the death of the nightwatchman. He did not bother to mention his attempted resignation when he made his statement; and when, soon after his second period of ninety days began, the commandant came to him in his cell to ask if he had tried to resign at some stage, Quick was surprised.

'Yes,' he said. 'Yes, I did once try to.'

'Why didn't you tell us that in your statement, Mr Quick?' asked the commandant.

'I didn't think it worthwhile,' said Quick. 'Anyway, how do you know that I did try to resign?'

'Mr Jeremy told us.'

'Oh,' said Quick. If Jeremy had told them, he must have told them a long time ago, he thought – there couldn't be anything very important in the question, then. He had not got up from his bed when the commandant came in and now he went back to the book that he was reading.

'Listen to me, Mr Quick,' said the commandant. 'Why did you try to resign?'

'Because I wanted to,' said Quick. He was still reading.

'Listen, Mr Quick, please. Your friend, Mr Jeremy. . . .'

'Dammit, he is not my friend.' Quick had been drawn from his book now.

'All right, Mr Quick. Mr Jeremy, who used to be your friend, told us that you tried to resign because you felt that the organization was going too far.'

'I tried to resign because I knew that I had made a mistake in ever joining the organization.'

'You thought that before you were detained, Mr Quick?'

'Yes. Oh hell, can't you go away and let me read? I've told you all I know. All I am waiting for now is for you to go away.'

'Listen, Mr Quick.' Quick did not look up from his book. 'Mr Quick, you don't seem to understand me. I want to know why you wanted to resign. Don't you understand, man? Pretoria has told me to find this out; there is just a chance, Mr Quick, that Pretoria may decide that you should not be charged.'

Quick looked up. 'You mean ...' he began, then stopped. He knew that he should not believe anything that the police said to him; everything they did was done to trap him. He dare not believe that the commandant was telling the truth – he was lying, he had to be lying.

'Yes, Mr Quick,' said the commandant. 'I mean that there is a chance that you will be released and that you will not be charged at all.'

'You're lying,' said Quick. 'You must be lying.'

'Why should I lie? Why, Mr Quick?' He did not look at Quick; his eyes seemed concerned only with the names and dates chipped on the cell walls.

'I don't know why you are lying, commandant. But you are lying. You are trying to trap me.'

'Why should I trap you? Come, Mr Quick, do you really think that I am anxious to send a man who is not completely guilty to the dock? If it is true that you tried to resign, there is a chance that Pretoria may decide that you should not be charged – mind, I am not making a promise, I tell you only that there is a chance. When I found out that you had tried to resign, I recommended to Pretoria that you should be released and should not be charged; Pretoria told me that if you would make a statement confirming that you tried to resign, they would consider my recommendation. Now will you tell me why you tried to resign?'

Three days after he had made the statement they transferred him to Sea Point police cells; the commandant told him then, and then again three weeks later, that Pretoria was still considering his statement. 'But there is a chance, I am not promising anything, but there is a chance, Mr Quick,' said the commandant.

Quick was released on 9 November. The trial of the rest of the Cape Town group began on 10 November. The charge was, at first, manslaughter and sabotage; most people had expected it to be murder and sabotage but, perhaps because the nightwatchman had not been white, the prosecution did not press the manslaughter charge – and on the second day the charge was reduced to sabotage only. The accused were Devis and Stevens; the chief witness for the state was Jeremy.

Part Two

The Houses are Burning

Sometimes, long afterwards, when Quick acted God in his own mind, he wished that he could make it end there; that was easy enough, that part of it – you had your lucky ones, those who got away, Hunter and Roseman and the not quite so lucky Quick; you had your heroes, Devis and Stevens; and you had your traitor, Jeremy. But Quick was still obsessed with the personal honour which he, though no one else, thought had been compromised in some way; so he knew that tidy explanations failed – objectively, he had behaved well; he'd made his statement but so had the heroes; he had escaped a gaol sentence but so had Hunter and Roseman – subjectively, he had failed in some way which only he could understand and which even he could not understand completely. This much he did know, that if you take as your moral norm action and action only, and when that action leads to death, you are denying what every man like him had to believe, that what is important in the end is that a man should choose to live rather than choose to die.

9

For the first four months after his release from detention, Quick was more or less mad, or so he realized afterwards.

He had the news that he was to get his belongings ready for a move from the Sea Point police cells in the middle of an afternoon on a day that he was fairly sure was Friday; and, because the commandant had told him that there was a chance of his being released, he was sure that this at last was the moment which his imagination had become centred on – not freedom, not fresh air, not a swim in the ice-cold Atlantic sea, not a good meal and a bath, but the moment at which he was going to insist that the police, after releasing him, take him back to the place where they had arrested him, to the door of what used to be Jeremy's flat. They were not, he had determined, going to sign the chit releasing him, shake hands with him, and then let him walk out of the door of the police station, so that he would have to stand on the pavement deciding whether to phone for a taxi or to take a bus back to his flat; they were bloody well going to drive him in a Security police car right back to Jeremy's front door. He wanted, almost, an acknowledgement that the police had stolen four months out of his life, an admission that they were putting him down where they had taken him from, even though they could not return those months.

So, when they did not release him that day, it took him a little time to realize that the moment had not come. The men who came to Sea Point to take him out were not any of the policemen who had been involved in questioning him – they were strangers and they refused to talk to him. They put him and his belongings in the car and they drove him away; the sergeant who had signed the removal order called out to him, 'Good luck, Mr Quick,' and Quick had to fight to keep his hand from waving a friendly good-bye. They are going to release me at Caledon Square, he thought, because that's the headquarters of the Security police. Then I'll ask to be taken back to the front door of Jeremy's flat.

But the driver did not turn off at Caledon Square; and Quick realized that they were probably going to release him at Woodstock, where he had been first detained. But to make sure, he leaned forward from the back seat, where he was sitting alone, and said, 'Are we going to Woodstock?' Neither of the policemen replied, so he said again, 'We are going to Woodstock, are we?' Still there was no reply and again he said, loudly this time, 'Look, you are going to release me at Woodstock, are you?'

'Shut up,' said the younger and the elder, more experienced but still as full of hate as his colleague, said, 'No talking, Mr Quick. We are not on your case, you know.' And they did not take the turning off the main road to the inland suburbs. Well, it's going to be Wynberg, I suppose, thought Quick; that's the police station closest to where they arrested me. But still the car did not turn off and Quick realized that they must be on the way to Parow; and he remembered that was where they kept all those whom they had finished with, those who had nothing more to tell that the police cared to hear; there, you awaited trial, not charged, still in detention, but awaiting trial all the same.

Suddenly panic closed itself around him, making the car stink with the smell of his own body – they were going to charge him after all, that was why they had sent policemen he didn't know, they were there just to transfer him to another cell, you wouldn't need the regulars to transfer you, you would need them only if you were going to be released. 'It's a mistake, it's a mistake,' he said out loud and made a move towards opening the car window, as if to let his fear escape. But the younger policeman, not driving, had half-turned when Quick spoke aloud and seeing Quick's hand going towards the door, he grabbed it and pulled it away. 'None of that stupid stuff, you,' he said.

'I was only trying to open the window; I'm hot,' said Quick but the policeman was not content. 'You just sit there in the middle of the seat, you, and I'll open the window,' he said.

But the fear did not leave Quick; for the first time since the police had taken him he was completely afraid. Up to that moment, he had not bothered to face the fact that he could spend fifteen years in prison – now he had to face it, now there was no escaping into theory and argument, now the judge's face loomed large in his images of horror. If you went to Parow you would be charged – everyone knew that; and if you were charged you would be tried and if you were tried there was a fair certainty that you would be convicted; oh, you could still be acquitted, but if the police thought you would be acquitted they would not bother to charge you. They must be sure, thought Quick, that they had enough on me to get me for a good long stretch – there wouldn't be any question of a token sentence; they would get him for five years at least. And where, before, he had been watching the outside world from the back seat of the police-car, thinking that however much he hated that world, he would soon be a part of it again, part of the world that walked up and down pavements looking in shop windows, part of the world that had gone on in much the same way without him, part of the breathing, unhappy, aimless, private, and very beautiful world, he now grew back into his detained self, tightly held by no active force in the middle of the back seat of a police-car, unable even to choose to try to escape, unable to see the town and the people outside the car as having any relation to him at all.

The next twenty-four hours were the worst of his whole detention; it was then that he lost hold of the small ledge he had made for himself on the cliff face. Even when Sergeant van Breda came to him that night to see that he was comfortably installed in his new cell, he was falling; even when the sergeant told him not to worry because the move was only a matter of shortage of cells near Caledon Square and was nothing to do with the police's changing their minds, he was falling; and by the time he was told, four o'clock the next afternoon, that he was to be released in an hour's time, he had fallen too far to be excited at the prospect of finding a new ledge.

The commandant himself came to sign the order releasing Quick – and before he signed it, he asked whether he could phone Quick's parents to ask them to fetch him from Parow; but when Quick said, 'No, thank you,' the commandant offered, before Quick had time to think of insisting, to drive him wherever he wanted. By now it seemed ridiculous to insist on being driven back to Jeremy's flat, where no one would be. So he accepted the offer and asked to be driven home. There was no talk in the car, partly because Quick could not bring himself to believe that the police were not trying yet another trick to damage him and partly because he knew, if the commandant was really intending to take him home and to leave him there, if the order to release was not just another police technique of softening his will, that he should thank him for having recommended his release – and he was not sure how to do it.

In the end, he avoided his difficulty by saying nothing when he got out of the police-car at his parent's house; he took his belongings and shut the door of the car without saying a word – and it was not until three years later, when he heard that the commandant had been compulsorily retired from the police force, that he regretted his decision; and it was not a great regret, for by then Quick had decided that qualms of conscience were, to any but those who called themselves liberals and were prepared to face the inevitable paradox implied by that, simply luxuries. You chose one side or the other, Quick decided; or you got out, as he had done; and to get out was no more than a refusal to choose finally.

His father and step-mother were out, for which Quick was glad; he was greeted by his five-year-old brother, Peter, who treated his appearance as entirely normal except for Quick's short prison beard, which he insisted must be shaved off immediately; he came to stand in the bathroom as Quick did it and he issued orders about how it should be done. Peter knew that his brother had been in prison, he said so, but he did not seem to find it frightening or even strange; he'd met other people who had been in gaol, he played often with the son of a white Communist who was serving a long sentence for incitement – and Peter's casual acceptance of the situation was good for Quick. He was not tempted to dramatize his feelings, he simply got on with what had to be done first, which was to get rid of the beard and the clothes and the dirt of four months in police cells. Annie, the servant, was equally casual; for her too, gaol was not an experience that people did not suffer regularly – she took Quick's clothes from outside the bathroom, found him some clean clothes, and then set about making him something special to eat; that was the only sign she gave of an awareness of the event.

Quick lay in his bath and talked to Peter, not of anything except what it was like to have a beard, why he had grown a beard, whether it hurt when it was cut off, why he hadn't let the beard cover his cheeks, why hair didn't grow on his forehead. Then, later, he sat in his parents' drawing-room and Peter gave him a drink, as formally as if he had been any other guest arriving when parents were out and when small boys do what they knew their parents would have done. So, by the time that Mr and Mrs Quick did arrive, Quick himself had grown to accept the fact of his detention so much in the way that Peter did that he was, at first, almost puzzled that his stepmother cried. He let her pamper him, let her bring him another drink, let her put pillows behind his head, let her bring him a sandwich, and then made her sit down beside him to be herself comforted and reassured. His father, meanwhile, fetched from his study a folder of all the press-cuttings about the detentions; he put it down beside Quick as if to say, Look, I really can't say it, but I cared terribly, and Quick understood and although he did not really care to know what the papers had said while he was inside, he read through all the cuttings, carefully, commenting, asking questions, being interested. Then his father phoned all Quick's friends and all his friends so that they would know before the papers; and when the papers did telephone to ask for interviews and comments, he refused to let them talk to Quick himself and insisted that the only statement they should try to get was one from the police about why they had detained his innocent son.

Yet Quick was mad and, afterwards, knew that he had been mad; if he had not been mad he would not have allowed his family to make a cotton-wool landing for him. If he had not been mad, he would have broken down, would have got roaring drunk and cried, would have done anything except sit with his family, eating and drinking and talking quietly. Even when Henry Naude brought Mary to see him he did not show any feeling; and it was four months later that he cried for the first time properly, cried for his friends and for himself, cried for the hopeless and corrupt world which he had fallen into. After that the nightmares had started, dreams of pursuit and capture, of hunters setting fire to the forests to drive the game out, of buildings falling down with fire breaking from their windows and always with him, or Devis, or Stevens, or Jeremy, trapped inside; and he had known then that he was sane again.

10

Most of his friends never mentioned Jeremy to Quick. Everyone knew that he had been released soon after the Cape Town trial had ended; after the judge had said that Jeremy was, as far as he and 'every other decent person' were concerned, at least as guilty as the friends he had given evidence against and without even the moral courage to stand by them, let alone his beliefs, 'however wrong they were'; that he hoped that Jeremy would have the sense to leave South Africa after the trial was over since no one of any opinion would be prepared to have anything to do with him; and that he was a disgrace not only to his country but to all who shared his opinions. But he was released, because the police had promised him indemnity if he gave evidence – and he had given it clearly and well, standing in the witness box, facing across the court at Stevens and Devis, naming them by their first names, and only once, when he was asked to recount the details of his arrest, showing any sign of breaking down. He had turned to the judge to say, 'Must I answer that question?'

'Yes, you must,' said the judge. 'I may remind you that you have been offered indemnity if you give evidence – that means that you cannot refuse to answer any question which is asked, unless of course it does not concern the case. The question does and so you must answer it.' So Jeremy had answered it and, half-way through, when he was telling how the police had found on the desk the sheets of instructions on how to lay charges and fuses – he had been carefully drilled by the police because he did not mention Hunter's name – he suddenly began to cry, not loudly, but almost as though he was being shaken by some deep, deathly cough; and it had taken everyone in the court a few moments to realize that he was crying. Then he had straightened his back, looked at the accused, and, as if he had not been in court at all, had said, 'Will you forgive me? Please forgive me, please forgive me, I still believe all that I used to believe, both of you please,' all in one breath so that what he said sounded almost ludicrous to the people in the court; and the court was called to order and Jeremy told to control himself and he had done so and he had answered the next question in the same low controlled voice that he used throughout the rest of the trial. Even when he was cross-examined by the defence lawyers, and when they tried to break him down again on the same question, he had not faltered.

Quick did not ever mention Jeremy's name, even to his father – he did not even think about why Jeremy had broken so quickly or about why he had given evidence for the state. Although he was in a situation in which to be rational could not possibly work, he was trying to be rational; and his attempt meant that questions which could not be answered could not be asked, even to himself. Mr Quick, who thought that he understood what was happening inside his son's head, tried once to force him to think about Jeremy; he asked Quick why Jeremy had left the documents next to his bed when he must have known that they and they alone were enough to convict him of sabotage. But Quick only shook his head and said, 'I don't know, I really don't know'; and when his father pressed him for an answer, he went on denying that any explanation was necessary; he did not want to think about it, he wanted to treat the Jeremy whom he had known and the Jeremy who had given evidence against Stevens and Devis as separate people.

Mary Dobling was the next person to try to get him to talk about Jeremy and, because Quick now needed Mary much more than he had done before, he tried to answer her. At first, he tried to explain Jeremy's actions by saying that he had somehow wanted to be a martyr; but he himself knew, as he went on, that it was an inadequate explanation – for, though a desire for martyrdom might explain why Jeremy had broken so soon, even why he had kept the documents next to his bed where they were bound to be found, it would not explain why he turned state evidence. That explanation would work only if you decided that Jeremy wanted to be on neither the side of the angels nor of the devils, but caught somewhere between them, caught as an Adam was trapped into destroying, not himself, but everything that made him seem lovely – and that too was not enough for Quick, because he could not or would not believe in original sin. It goes deeper than that, thought Quick, it goes deeper even than personal geography; and when he got there, he could not, in his present rationalism, go any further. So he fell back on the idea that the Jeremy he had known had somehow died and that the person with whom he had been arrested had been someone whom he did not know, someone who had taken over Jeremy's body but nothing else of his.

'You don't understand at all, do you?' said Mary to him when she heard him flounder in his explanation. 'Really, you don't understand, do you?'

'I think I understand as well as anyone,' said Quick. 'I understand as well as you do, don't I?'

'No,' said Mary. 'No, you don't at all.'

'All right, you tell me what you understand.'

'You've missed out all along the line, Donald – you don't understand at all.'

'It's no good telling me that – tell me what I have missed out.'

'I can't do that, Donald. If you can't see it yourself, you won't see it when I explain.'

'Dammit, don't be so vague – give me reasons, tell me what I've missed.'

But Mary would not – she implied only that he was, in his present state of mind, incapable of understanding; and Quick, though he did not believe that he was, was still glad to drop the conversation and be content with Mary's claim that he did not understand, because he thought that really he did. So he went on believing that there were two Jeremys, one who had been his friend and one who was now his enemy.

But most of his friends never mentioned Jeremy to Quick, so, unable to talk about Jeremy to the one person who had been, as everyone agreed, the closest to him, they all began to do what Quick did, which was to treat the old Jeremy as being now dead or, at any rate, a ghost. They heard about him but they treated the reports as they might have done reports of a revolution in some country the whereabouts of which they were not sure; they heard that, after his release, he had gone back to stay with his parents, they heard that he had seen Sheilagh Owen, that he had asked her to marry him, and that she had refused – no one knew why because no one, not even Mary, saw Sheilagh any more – they heard that, as a condition of his release, Jeremy had to report once a week to a police station – they heard that he had gone to stay with friends on the coast of Natal, they heard that he had come back to Cape Town to stay with his mother and father again, and they heard that he had decided not to leave South Africa. When they heard that, Jeremy for a moment seemed a real person again, for all of them believed that to be the crucial decision facing any white South African, whether to leave South Africa or not. The rights and wrongs of exile were always in their minds; and it was part of the way their minds worked that they should assume that it was moral to leave South Africa if you were in serious political trouble, if, for instance, you faced a prison sentence by staying.

Jeremy had decided to stay; if he had not been a traitor, they would, most of them, have applauded his decision, even if they did not suppose that they themselves would be able to do what they called 'stick it out' – which meant, mainly, learn to live with the conscience that white liberals were bound to have, a conscience created by the fact that, because they were white, they lived well, even when they were in the most serious political trouble possible – because, even in prison, a white man was treated better than a black man, got better food, more books, a more comfortable cell, less brutality, more visitors. They all knew that; what they did not know was how you came to terms with it, how to learn to accept the privilege of birth even when you believed that it was a wrong privilege – and few of them saw that it was not a particularly local problem. But how could anyone say that Jeremy had decided to stick it out, they wondered; could a traitor be supposed to stick out the consequences of his treachery? In the end, most of them decided that he should have left the country – and the few who did not argued simply that it showed the woolliness of the opposition, the real not the parliamentary opposition, that Jeremy had not been executed by his former friends for having become a traitor. Yet if any one of them had been given the means of killing Jeremy, he would not have done so and knew and said that he could not do so, 'not in cold blood, anyway', they said, as if hotbloodedness would excuse political murder.

But Jeremy's little gust of life did not last long; he was, though he lived in the same town, as good as in exile. The terrible thing was, said Henry Naude, that it was not simply Jeremy who seemed unreal now; it was also Devis and Stevens – not of course that any of them had known Stevens very well. But Devis, taken forcibly out of their circle of friends, seemed little more alive than Jeremy did; and the letters Naude wrote to Devis in gaol, the food parcels that Devis's university friends clubbed together to buy for him, and the occasional reference made to him in university speeches and pamphlets were little more than offerings to the dead, coins to weight his eyelids down, and flowers to mask the fresh earth over his coffin. And Henry Naude, realizing this but not daring to tell anyone, tried to make up for his lack of feeling by writing, not only to Devis, but to Jeremy, offering to do anything for him that he needed. That was the first move anyone made towards taking Jeremy back – Mr and Mrs Jeremy had, of course, never let go of him; and no one, not even Jeremy's parents, knew of the other person who had not let go either.

Jeremy did not reply to Naude's letter for some time, such a time in fact that Henry began to think that perhaps he had been mistaken in writing at all. But, after nearly two months, a reply did come, a reply which said only that Jeremy appreciated Henry's offer but that, for the time being, he thought that they should not meet; 'I shall almost certainly need your help some time,' wrote Jeremy, 'but I'd prefer, if you don't mind, to wait until I feel more able to face you and the others.' Henry, who had not suggested in his letter that they should meet, only that he would be prepared to help Jeremy, was at first annoyed that Jeremy should have interpreted his letter as a suggestion that they should meet; but later he decided that it must be a just interpretation and was profoundly glad that Jeremy had not wanted to meet him – for, however disturbed he was that he should feel that those who had passed outside the knowledge of his senses should seem unreal, the fact was that he did still think of Jeremy in that way.

It was, as Quick said, almost as if Jeremy had died.

II

It took Quick four months to start realizing his nightmares; it took him another four to find the courage to leave his parents' home for a place of his own again. He had started work again only a fortnight after his release and his editor, either because he was anxious to keep the paper out of serious police trouble or because he was anxious about the state of Quick's health, at first kept him off any but the most ordinary reporting; Quick was not asked to write anything remotely political, and more and more became responsible for sub-editing the weekly magazine section of the paper, phoning up fashionable ladies to get their comments on the latest styles, editing letters for the family page, writing a few reviews, anything that had nothing to do with what he knew best. But every evening he would go back from his newspaper retreat to his family hiding-place; he would not go out, he would not go to meetings, the cinema, the theatre, exhibitions, anything, he wanted to stay at home – it was not that he did not welcome friends who came to see him, for he often saw Henry Naude and, of course, Mary; but they had to see him and they would sit in his parents' drawing-room and talk for as long as they could; but there was so much Henry dared not mention to Quick, that, without the kind of chatter that would have been provided by a setting which he was more used to, a student café or a bar or a party, Henry Naude would find that, after half an hour, they were both sitting there, looking at the walls, not saying anything even trivial; and then he would try to persuade Quick to come out with him, to go to a party or to a bar, and when Quick refused, Henry would force himself to stay another half-hour before he would leap up to say, 'I must go now, I must go.' So Mary Dobling would come to see him too and it seemed that his parents did not mind that he took her up to his bedroom to make love to her; and after they had finished they would lie on the bed and share three or four cigarettes and sometimes Quick would try to talk to Mary but it usually did not work – she was never much good at talking. So Quick would lean over her and would ask her what was wrong, because he knew at least that something was wrong when she could make love to him and afterwards not be able to say anything more than, 'I love you, Donald.' That seemed to be almost all that she could say to him; but though he suspected that Mary felt something that she would not tell him Quick was, in a way, content simply to know that she did love him – he had the physical expression of love, he had the statement of love, and besides those the small silences seemed unimportant to him.

It was not that Quick enjoyed those eight months at his home – enjoyment was not a word that applied at all for he had to stay there, there was a necessity for it that over-rode any pleasure or dislike. After the first four months he was self-conscious enough to know that he needed the cottonwool of his family; he enjoyed having meals at the same time each day, he enjoyed being able to talk to his father about the books he reviewed each week, he enjoyed his stepmother's affection and his small brother's hero-worship, but all these were separate, they did not add up to the statement, 'I am staying with my parents because they make me comfortable', or even, 'I am staying with my parents because they love me'. He stayed there because it provided him with four fixed walls, as a police cell had done, because there was no need to argue with anyone even when they disagreed, and because they could say as much by keeping quiet as they could by talking.

But after eight months it was time to go; the cotton-wool was beginning to suffocate, the routine to seem tedious, and the quietness stupidity. At first he looked for a place of his own, a small cottage or a pre-war flat near his work; but then Henry Naude suggested that Quick move in to live with him, in the flat he had kept on his own since Devis had been arrested more than a year before. Quick accepted – he liked Henry, they had grown close during the time since the trial, and Henry seemed to be both casual and unmuddled in the way he lived.

That step taken, the rest was easy; with Mary to coax him and with Henry to protect him, with his job to force him into making some kind of contact with people he did not know very well, Quick began to re-establish his university friendships; Henry Naude, Mary, Koos Reisman, and he would often go to parties together, or would go off with a group of friends to a political meeting at the university or would drive, on a Sunday, out into the country where no one could look disturbed at the sight of three young whites in the company of a coloured man eating out of the same sandwich packets and drinking out of the same beer bottles.

Once, even, at a meeting organized to call for the repeal of the law under which he and other members of the organization had been detained, Quick made a short speech, saying that, as someone who had experienced the effects of solitary confinement, he urged that the legislation be repealed. Not everyone could hear what he said, for the hall was very crowded, but everyone agreed that it was courageous of him to risk bringing the police down on him again by saying so openly how terrible solitary confinement was. After that, Quick found that he could talk easily about what it had been like; he still found it necessary, however, to refuse an invitation to speak at the university on the effects of solitary confinement – it was all right with friends, or even with people he hardly knew, but it seemed somehow impossible that he should actually have to organize his reactions into a coherent whole so that he could explain to a formal audience what it had been like. But I am all right now, he would think; the damage has been repaired – I can live like a normal person again; and he even began to work out an article for his newspaper on the effects of solitary detention and wrote an amusing but frightening account of everything that had happened up to the moment he had been handcuffed to Jeremy. But he could not get any further than that and, though he made notes, he was forced to decide that the article would have to wait until he was able to see the events from a further distance than a year.

12

The first person who tried to make Quick see Jeremy was Mrs Jeremy. She came to the flat one Sunday morning, when Henry Naude was still in bed and Quick, in pyjamas, was wandering about the flat drinking coffee and looking at the Sunday newspapers – when Mrs Jeremy knocked on the door, Quick thought that it must be Mary come to see him; she had left him the night before earlier than usual; she had been tired, she had said, and did not want to go out anyway – perhaps she's come round now to try to make amends for having gone off so early yesterday, thought Quick; but when he opened the door it was Mrs Jeremy.

She did not say anything and Quick, for a moment, did not recognize her. When he did, all he said was, 'What do you want?' He did not ask her in nor did he apologize for being still in pyjamas; he did not even dare to call her by her name.

'I want to see you, Donald. May I come in, please?'

For a moment Quick thought that he might have the courage to refuse. But as he hesitated, she moved past him and into Naude's bedroom. 'You can't go in there,' said Quick, but she was already in. Naude rolled over under his pile of blankets and looked to see who it was. 'Who are you?' he said; he was obviously angry at being woken so early on a Sunday morning. Mrs Jeremy did not answer him but turned to Quick. 'Isn't there somewhere we can go to talk, Donald?' she asked.

'What about?' asked Naude from his bed. Now that he was awake he wanted to know what was going on.

Mrs Jeremy looked at him for a few seconds before replying; she was making up her mind whether or not to be rude, Quick knew – and he hoped that she would be, because she would expect Naude to be quelled by it, and he would not be, almost at any time, but especially on a Sunday morning. But Mrs Jeremy did not reply sharply; she smiled at Naude and said, 'About my son – James Jeremy.'

Naude sat up in bed, pulling the bedclothes up as he did so. 'Are you Mrs Jeremy?' he said, almost stupidly.

'Yes, I am. Are you surprised to see me here? Are you a friend of my son's?'

Before Naude could answer, Quick cut in. 'He used to be a friend of Jeremy,' he said coldly.

Mrs Jeremy seemed not to get the implication of what Quick said, for she smiled at Naude and said, 'I'm sorry to disturb your rest – but I was anxious to see Donald. May I ask who you are?'

Again Quick answered for Henry. 'He's Henry Naude – he used to live here with Arthur Devis.'

'Oh yes, of course. I've heard your name often.'

'Have you?' said Henry. 'I hope it was complimentary.'

'I think that it was – it was James who told me about you. He seems to like you very much.'

'Does he?' said Henry. He was wide awake now, watching this tall, attractive woman, entirely at her ease apparently; and Quick suddenly hated her for that, for that and for being Jeremy's mother. 'We really can't stand here making social noises,' he burst out. 'Mrs Jer . . .' he choked over the name and slurred it over, 'Perhaps you'd better come into my room or into the kitchen to tell me whatever you want, unless you want to tell me in front of Henry.'

'I don't mind where I tell you what I want,' she said. 'But perhaps I would embarrass you less in another room than Mr Naude's.'

'I'm sure that you won't embarrass me,' said Henry, 'unless of course I embarrass you. I can't offer to go into another room because, you see, I haven't any clothes on.'

'I can see that,' said Mrs Jeremy, and she smiled at Henry.

Again Quick burst out, 'For God's sake come next door, and leave Henry to his sleep.'

'All right, Donald. Shall we go into the kitchen? Perhaps I can have a cup of coffee? I seem to remember that you make very good coffee.' She turned away from Henry and followed Quick out of the room, looking back to smile at Henry, who was still sitting up in bed.

In the kitchen, Quick made her a cup of coffee, gave her milk, offered her sugar, and then sat down on the kitchen table. She pulled a stool from under the table and sat down, crossing her legs carefully and smoothing her skirt down.

'Well?' said Quick. He did not look at her.

'It's quite simple, Donald. I would like you to come to see Jeremy.'

'Did he ask you to come to see me?' Quick still did not look at her.

'No, he didn't, in fact. But I think that it would be good for him to see you again. He hasn't seen you for months now.'

'The last time I saw Jeremy was when I was arrested outside his flat and that is more than a year now.'

'Yes, I suppose it is. Will you come to see him?'

'Why does he want to see me?'

'He hasn't said that he wants to see you – I simply think that he would like to see you.'

'And it doesn't matter that I don't want to see him?'

'Why don't you want to see him?'

Now Quick looked at her – he was sure of what he had to say. He could not allow this, he could not allow anything that suggested that Jeremy was a real person. 'Do I have to spell it out to you?' he said. 'I regard Jeremy as a traitor; I have no desire to have anything to do with traitors of any kind.'

'James did not betray you, Donald. He tried to protect you.'

'Oh, nonsense. Did he tell you that?' He was standing now, looking out of the kitchen window. From where he stood, he could see most of Table Mountain; the air was very clear that morning and it looked as if you could walk up the mountain in a few minutes, just a little stroll over most of the Cape peninsula, over Robben Island, and miles of the Atlantic, the sea, the land, the mountain, all at your feet.

Mrs Jeremy was talking; he had not heard what she said. 'Sorry,' he interrupted. 'I wasn't listening. Will you say that again?'

'I said that Jeremy was the one who told the police that you tried to resign from the organization after the nightwatchman was killed.'

'I know that,' said Quick. 'I'm not particularly grateful, you know.'

'You should be, shouldn't you? After all it saved you a long time in prison.'

'It saved me from going to the prison that Jeremy would have been happy to send me to. Do you really think that he would have given evidence against Stevens and Devis and not against me?' Quick was almost laughing at her; the idea that Jeremy believed that he had tried to save him was ludicrous to him. 'Really, you can tell Jeremy that I don't think that I am in his debt at all for having told the police that. If it hadn't been for him, for his having kept those things next to his bed, for his being prepared to tell the police what he knew, none of us would have got into trouble at all. He's a fool if he believes that I am grateful to him.'

'I thought that you were a friend of his, Donald.'

'I used to be a friend; I am not any more. To tell the truth, I hate Jeremy, I would be glad to see him dead, I would be even more glad to see him in the place he put Stevens and Arthur, rotting in a cell somewhere.' Quick was still very much in control of his voice; it seemed to creep around the kitchen like the voice of someone outside the room, it was so quiet, so flat.

'He didn't do anything to harm you, Donald, not really. And even if he hadn't turned evidence, Stevens and Devis would have still gone to gaol – what James did made no difference at all, it meant only that one person less went to prison.'

Suddenly rage, like a drunken bird, flew wildly into Quick's mind. 'Damn you,' he shouted, 'Why should Jeremy be the one who did not go to gaol? Why should he have the right to decide that he should not go but that Devis and Stevens should? Did you give him that right? Did you?'

'He wasn't the only one who didn't go to gaol – you didn't go, Roseman didn't, and there was someone else too, wasn't there, someone who escaped? I don't know his name but there was someone else, wasn't there? None of you went to gaol. Why should you blame James for not going?'

Quick looked at her across the room – she seemed to believe what she was saying, and he could not believe that; she must know how wrong she was, she must, he thought. 'Don't you understand?' he said. 'It isn't Jeremy's not going to prison that I mind; what I do mind is that he told the police what he knew and then went and gave evidence against his friends. He's a traitor, don't you understand, a traitor?'

'He didn't betray you. It was that man who sold the explosives who did. James isn't a traitor, he still believes everything that he used to believe.'

'Listen to me, damn you. He sent his friends to gaol, he stood there in the witness box and he told everything that they had done, he looked straight at them and he sent them to gaol. If he isn't a traitor, then I am mad.' Quick was screaming at her now, without realizing that he was; and Naude came into the kitchen, with a blanket around him, and stood in the doorway looking at Quick. 'Calm down, Donald, for heaven's sake. You'll have the neighbours phoning the police again,' he said. 'What on earth have you been talking about to make Donald behave like this, Mrs Jeremy?'

'Christ, Henry, that woman is trying to persuade me Jeremy isn't a traitor, that to give evidence against your friends doesn't necessarily make you a traitor. She wants me to see Jeremy, she wants me to shake hands with him and say, "All's forgiven, old chap. I don't mind that you gave state evidence. I would have done exactly the same thing in your place." Well, I bloody well won't. I won't see your son, do you hear that? I wish that he were dead, I wish that I had never met him, I wish never to hear his name again.'

'Calm down, Donald,' Henry repeated. 'Is that really what you said, Mrs Jeremy? Did Jeremy send you here?'

'James did not send me here and all I asked was that Donald should come to see him again.'

'Well, I won't come, I won't.' Quick was shouting at her again, letting all that he felt beat out of the cage of his mind and into the air.

'Donald, shut up,' said Henry. 'Really, Mrs Jeremy. I don't

think that it was very wise of you to come here, particularly if Jeremy didn't ask you to come.'

'I don't think, Mr Naude,' she said and now she stood up, 'that it is your business to tell me whether or not my actions for my son's sake are wise.'

Henry's voice was very polite; 'I did not intend to be impertinent, Mrs Jeremy. But it should be fairly obvious that you are not going to persuade Donald to see him.'

'Will you really not see him?' She turned to Quick again and suddenly all the pride, the arrogance of certainty and charm, were gone and she seemed very tired and very desperate.

'No,' said Quick and he hesitated, then said again, 'No. I won't see him, I can't see him, and you should not even ask me that.'

'Are you sure?' asked Henry.

'Whose side are you on, Henry? Do you want me to kiss and make up too?' asked Quick.

'You know which side I'm on, Donald, or you should do.' Henry was smiling at Quick; then he turned to Mrs Jeremy and said, 'I think that you are wasting your time, Mrs Jeremy. I don't think that Donald wants to see Jeremy,' and he smiled again, this time at his own understatement.

Mrs Jeremy did not smile back at him. She took her handbag from the kitchen table and walked to the doorway from the kitchen into the hall. There she stopped and turned back to look at Quick; her head was thrown back again now, her shoulders set again in the pugnacious self-assurance she had had before her last appeal, and she said, 'Oh, Donald, tell me, do you still see much of that charming girl Mary? Mary Dobling, I think her name is.'

'Yes, I do. Why do you ask?' said Quick. Suddenly he hated her again, suddenly all the pity that had made him hesitate before he said no finally was gone, and he wanted only that she should take herself away from him. 'What's it to do with you?' he asked again, deliberately making his question as rude as he could.

'No particular reason,' smiled Mrs Jeremy at him. 'I just

wanted to know – she seemed a most interesting girl when I met her. Good-bye, Donald; I am sorry to have disturbed you so much,' and she turned to Henry, 'and to have disturbed your Sunday morning sleep,' and then she left, Henry holding open the front door for her with one hand while his other clutched the blanket around him.

The next person who tried was Quick's father. One evening, late, when they were sitting on the verandah of the Quicks' house in Mowbray, having a last drink before Quick went back to the flat, his father turned to him and said, 'Don't you think, Donald, that it is time you saw James Jeremy again?'

The question was completely unexpected; his father had given no warning that he was thinking of anything like that, they had been talking of other things, of Mr Quick's teaching, of a film they had been to see at a local film society, of an exhibition of painting that Quick had reviewed for the newspaper; and Quick could not answer his father for a moment or two, he was so surprised by the question. He was not angry, he very seldom was with his father, he was simply surprised.

'Why on earth should you suggest that now, Dad?' asked Quick.

'Oh, I just thought that perhaps you should make some effort to see James Jeremy.'

'But why?'

'No reason in particular – I just thought it would be a good idea.'

'Dad, has someone suggested this to you? It's not your own idea, is it?'

'Oh, no, nobody suggested it to me.'

'Come off it, Dad, you're a hopeless liar. You didn't think yourself that I should see Jeremy, did you? Where did you get the idea from?'

Mr Quick laughed – it was true, he was not a good liar. Like most schoolmasters, he preferred to tell the truth, even when it was rude truth; and like most schoolmasters, he thought that the truth was usually simple, something that could be stated without fear of the consequences. So he said, 'All right – I'm not supposed to tell you, but it isn't my idea. Mrs Jeremy came to see your step-mother and me a few days ago; she asked me to persuade you to see James Jeremy again.'

'And your wife – what about her? Did she think that it was a good idea?'

'Oh, you know her – she doesn't forgive easily, especially when she thinks that someone has hurt one of us.'

'And she thinks that Jeremy hurt me? Don't you think that too? Don't you think that he hurt me?'

'In a way, I think so – but not badly, Donald, really, not as badly as he hurt himself.'

'And what about the others, Stevens and Devis? Don't you think that he hurt them?'

'Obviously he did. But do you have the right to try to punish him because of what he did to them?'

'If people like me don't punish him, who will? Somebody has got to show him that he has passed to a place where no one decent will have anything to do with him.'

'You sound just like the judge must have sounded, Donald.'

'And don't you think that I'm right?'

Mr Quick got up from his deckchair; he walked over to the edge of the verandah and looked up into the night sky – it's almost as if he's praying, thought Quick; he loved his father very much at that moment, loved him not for wisdom nor for the certainty that he gave his family, but for his ability to doubt his own judgements. Quick got up from his chair too and walked over to join his father.

'It's a beautiful night, isn't it, Donald?' They stood there, looking up; there were so many stars out that you could not tell one from the other. 'Strange to think that some of the light we see now left long before I was born, even. I wonder, Donald. I wonder if you are right. I know that what he did seems inexcusable; but I wonder if we should blame him.' He shuddered suddenly. 'That mother of his, she is terrible, isn't she?'

'Yes, but I don't think that she can be blamed for her son's evil-doing.'

'No, of course not. "The sins of the fathers" – or mothers for that matter – shouldn't be visited, shouldn't be counted as visiting on their sons; that's too easy, isn't it? Yes, I believe in individual responsibility just as much as you do, Donald – but he is a friend of yours, isn't he? To some extent he's your responsibility, isn't he?'

'He's not my friend any more, Dad; I think that he stopped being a friend of mine a long time ago. But even if it's true that I share responsibility for him, I don't see why I particularly should take responsibility now, any more than I think you have to because we live in this terrible country.'

'Oh, I take responsibility for that, Donald – I go on living here although I do nothing to change things, although I hate what happens here. And just by being here I take responsibility, though I take it pretty lightly, I suppose.'

'And so, in the same way, just because I was once a friend of his, I take responsibility for all his actions, even after we are no longer friends? Is that what you think?'

'Yes, I suppose so, Donald. And obviously you don't agree.'

'No, I don't, Dad. I've not been a Christian for a long time now ...'

'There is more than one way of being a Christian,' his father interrupted gently.

'Perhaps, Dad; but I'm not a Christian in any way. I can't forgive Jeremy and it isn't even that I want to; I want to hate him. I believe that it is a political necessity to hate him.'

'Are you so sure that it is not simply a psychological necessity? Are you so sure that you don't hate him because you need to, for your own sake?'

Quick hesitated; his father's insights always weighed heavily with him, if only because they were so seldom stated as facts. But he was sure; forgiveness would be, in a way, the easy way out. He did not want to hate Jeremy, he had to hate him, not for himself, but for the others, and not simply for the others, for all those who would try to change the country and who would need to know that traitors were dealt with, if not physically, at least by ostracism.

'Yes, I am sure, Dad, I can't see James Jeremy, I really can't. It would be, in some ways, as bad as going into the witness box myself, going up there to stand next to him and to prompt him in sending Stevens and Devis to gaol.'

Mr Quick turned away from the verandah railing. He smiled at Donald. 'All right, son, if you are sure. Perhaps you are right, perhaps it would be betraying your other friends if you saw this one.' He sighed. 'I'll have to phone that woman in the morning to tell her, if you don't mind. God, I dislike her.'

'Will you tell her that you tried to persuade me?'

'No, of course not. I'll simply tell her that we talked about it and we decided that it would be better that you shouldn't. Is that all right?'

'Thank you, Dad.'

'Not at all, Donald – you are perhaps right about this business. I'm so far removed from politics these days. Did you know that I used to know Helena Jeremy in the old days, before I married your mother?'

'No, I didn't. Did you know her well?'

'Not really. She used to go out with some of my friends in those days – she was very beautiful, I suppose. I hated her – but I think that she may have turned out all right if only she could have met someone better than that poor little rich man.'

'But she wasn't the kind not to choose a man like that, was she?'

'No, I suppose not – still, I feel sorry almost for her now, poor woman.'

That was the end of it, apparently; for Mr Quick never mentioned to Donald what Mrs Jeremy had said when he phoned her and Donald never asked to know. He wanted only to forget Jeremy; but, all the same, what his father had said worked in his mind and, though he did not immediately change it, he began to see what he thought was a necessity for understanding – and both that necessity and his inability to understand meant that when he was next forced to think of meeting Jeremy again, he found that it was almost as if the decision had been taken for him already.

Especially, Quick decided that somehow he had to work out why Jeremy, of all people, had turned state witness – he had tried before but, now, when he discovered that he could not understand, he did not fall back on the idea that the Jeremy he had known and the Jeremy the traitor were two different people who happened to inhabit the same body. However, he could still not understand and so he decided that what had happened must be inexplicable – there was no logic of reasons that could be worked out. Oh, he knew that it was easy enough to break down in solitary confinement – he had done that himself: you took any person who depended for the unity inside him on things or people outside him away from those things, those people, and he would, immediately, or almost immediately, or after a little while, or even after quite a long time, break; and that meant that almost everyone would break – the only possible exceptions, thought Quick, were those whose interiors were so closely modelled on some exterior system that interior and exterior could not be distinguished – your exceptions were the believing chameleons, the saints and the fanatics; they might last or they might not, but they had a better chance than those who always doubted.

But the step from breaking down in solitary confinement, from that first stage of treachery when you told the police what you knew, to the last stage, when you stood up in a court room, when you actually faced your friends and, in a way, the whole of society, when you cut yourself off from all honour so completely, . . . well, for him that was not a step at all; it was a flight of stairs, it was a cliff, it was a whole range of mountains. What would remain inexplicable was that Jeremy should have taken that leap into treachery – oh, you could see some reasons for it, Quick knew: the unhappy home, the sexual mixup, the exhibitionism; but none of these alone was reason for what Jeremy had done. Indeed, not even the sum of all these things was enough, for in some way the sum seemed to be greater than the individual parts – yet that was, to Quick, intellectually unsatisfactory, if only because he should now be able to look back at the Jeremy he had known to say, Yes, I could have seen, if only I had looked closely enough; I could have seen all those things which together must inevitably have made a traitor.

Try as he might, Quick could not say this; he could not look back at Jeremy as he had been until that moment he was arrested to say, I should have guessed all along.

Yes, decided Quick, yes, it was inexplicable; yet in another way he knew that it was not enough to say that – for himself, for Devis, for Stevens, probably for Roseman, and perhaps most definitely of all for Hunter, the sum of the whole could not have been greater than the parts – you could put the parts together in any order you like and they still would not equal treachery of that kind. All of them, even Hunter, might have broken after some time; but he was sure that none of them would have turned state witness, whatever the temptations had been. Would he have turned state witness himself? He shied away from the thought as a horse might from a snake – he knew that he might have been tempted for a time, as even Devis had been; but he would not have been able to go through with it. But what was there special about Jeremy, he would try to think, what was there special that had meant that he was bound to break at the crucial time; what was it that would make all those weaknesses run together in a time of crisis? Was it what had seemed so special about Jeremy beforehand, that sort of nervy excitement that he had seemed to generate around all that he did? But that happened outside him – did it correspond to something inside him?

Again and again, Quick tried to imagine himself in the same situation as Jeremy had been in. Suppose he came from that kind of home, suppose he had been arrested in bed with Mary, suppose he had been keeping the papers next to his bed, suppose Mary's parents had been brought in to taunt him, suppose all else that had happened to Jeremy had happened to him, would he then have done what Jeremy had done? Oh, it might have helped break him more quickly, almost as quickly as Jeremy had done, but would it have been enough to make him give evidence against the others? Either he lacked the imagination to say of himself, Yes, that would have happened, or else it would not have happened – he would not have taken that final step into what was little more than a state of death. Indeed, that was how Quick saw himself – he was like a man searching a morgue for someone who he knew was dead, someone whose face he could only just remember, someone whom he had to find. But each face he looked at was the same; and each dead face seemed to take on the features of the man he had known.

So, whichever way he tried, he could not understand what had driven Jeremy into that act of despair. He could not understand – that was all. Yet, more and more, he felt it necessary to understand; it became almost as if he were searching for himself in that morgue. Why was it possible for someone who had once been his friend to have that weakness, when others whom he did not even like would not have behaved in the same way? Why was he so sure that Hunter would not have behaved in the same way? Was he so sure that he himself would not have turned state witness? He had to get some kind of answer, he knew. He had, therefore, to see Jeremy. Sooner or later, he was going to have to face him.

Yet still Quick could not decide completely – certainly he was not prepared to write to Jeremy to ask to see him; his anger with Mrs Jeremy was still too strong, his anger with, and his fear of, Jeremy himself were still too strong, and he could not take the decision – he needed time to become himself again. But the decision was in his mind; he decided that in a way it had been taken for him.

Koos Reisman did not ask Quick to see Jeremy although he went to see Jeremy himself. He did not tell anyone that Jeremy had written asking to see him, he did not tell anyone that he was going, and no one knew that he had been until after he had, mysteriously, disappeared.

A fortnight after his disappearance, he wrote a short note to Henry Naude – it was addressed from Francistown in Bechuanaland. 'As you will see from the address,' he wrote, 'I have skipped the country – I can't tell you why but I wanted you and the others to know that I was all right. It was surprisingly easy; what is not going to be so easy is to get away from this place – but I can tell you that I am heading, probably gradually, for London and I hope we shall meet there one day. My regards to Donald and Mary and any others you care to mention this news to; oh, and take my advice, keep away from James Jeremy – I went to see him shortly before I left and it was a mistake. I really can't tell you more than that.'

Henry was puzzled by the letter for he had not even suspected that Koos might have felt, like him, that they still owed Jeremy something. Koos had not, as far as he knew, been deeply involved in political action and he was surprised that Koos had not told him that he was going. So he showed the letter to Mary and asked her what she thought; but if she thought anything about it, she refused to tell him what and said only that she thought he should not show the letter to Quick.

All the same, despite Koos's warning, the next person who asked Quick to see Jeremy was Henry Naude. It was not that he did not treat the warning seriously, it was just that he was the kind of man who kept his promises, even when the circumstances in which he had made a promise had changed. He had promised his help to Jeremy and so he gave it.

It happened one Saturday night, at a party to which Quick had taken Mary; Henry arrived late, at about ten, and immediately he had gone over to where Quick and Mary were standing talking to a group of their university friends and had taken Quick away into a corner.

'I must talk to you, Donald,' he had said and, when they were where no one could eavesdrop, he said, 'I've done something that may upset you but I think that it was necessary. Are you feeling strong?'

'As strong as I ever do. Come, Henry, what's your secret? Do you want me to stay out of the flat tonight?'

'It's more serious than that. I want you, in fact, to go back to the flat right now.'

'But why? I'm enjoying myself here and I'm not misbehaving, not yet at any rate.'

'Because Jeremy is at the flat and he wants to see you.'

Quick stood looking at Henry for a long time before he answered. The room was very noisy; people were beginning to get drunk on the cheap red wine that the hosts had provided; in one corner a group of rugby-players were arguing about the afternoon's match and in another, the darkest one, a young man stood with his arms around two girls – Quick could see that though they were pretending to be talking, the man was in fact playing with their breasts; he wondered whether each girl knew that the other was being felt too – it did not seem at all indecent, it seemed almost proper, he thought.

Suddenly he turned back to Henry. 'Will you come with me?' he asked.

Henry shook his head. 'I think that you'd better go by yourself,' he said.

'And you think that I should go?'

'Yes.'

'So do I,' said Mary – Quick turned to her; he had not realized that she had been listening – she must have come up very quietly, he thought.

'Did you know that Jeremy wanted to see me?'

Mary shook her head.

'Will you come with me?' Quick asked her.

'No,' said Mary. 'I think Henry's right – if you are going to see him, you must go on your own.'

'How will you get home?'

'I'll wait here until you come back from seeing him – then you can take me home. And if you're very late, I'm sure that Henry will see me home safely, won't you, Henry?'

'Of course,' said Henry.

'All right,' said Quick. 'All right, I'll go to see him. I won't be long either, Mary, so you won't need to see her home, Henry; not of course that I don't trust you,' he added, grinning at Henry, who did not smile back.

13

Jeremy was waiting in the flat for him – he was sitting in the old casual attitude, one leg slung over the arm of his chair, head thrown back, fingers tapping impatiently on the table beside the chair. He did not get up to greet Quick, nor did he say anything; after a moment or two he stopped tapping, the better to concentrate on watching Quick standing in the doorway of the flat, looking across the room to Jeremy.

'Hullo,' said Quick. He did not move into the room.

Jeremy smiled but did not say anything. He looks at me, thought Quick, almost as if I were the one who had come calling, as if I were the new Quick who needed forgiveness. He savoured this thought but, to his surprise, it did not make him angry; he did not mind Jeremy's smile, his arrogant silence, his not standing. He was too curious to be angry, he supposed; and he felt almost pleased to see Jeremy again. Yes, he was pleased to see him. He wanted to hurry forward, wanted to shake hands with him, wanted to ask him hundreds of questions, wanted to sit where he could watch Jeremy's quick eyes; and this he knew should make him angry, for it was the reaction he had been most intent to avoid. But he was not angry, he knew – he was, simply, pleased to see Jeremy again.

Now he moved into the room; he did not go near Jeremy, all the same, but went over to the far side of the room to sit on Henry's bed. Steeled there, a pillow against the wall behind his head, he was ready.

'Were you so sure I would come?' he asked.

'I thought that you would; I wasn't sure but I thought that you would.'

'Why? I've refused before to see you.'

'Have you? I didn't know.'

Jeremy's reply was curiously flat and Quick wondered if he was telling the truth – should he test him out, he thought; should he ask if Jeremy did not know that his mother had tried very hard to get him to see her son? But it hardly seemed worthwhile – he wanted to ask Jeremy so many more important questions that a few lies at the start would not hurt. He found his cigarettes in his jacket pocket, took one for himself, lit it, and then made as if to throw the packet and the matches across to Jeremy.

'No thanks, Donald. I gave it up while I was inside.' He spoke as if he recognized the irony of the small self-denial having taken place in the greatest self-assertion but Quick ignored that.

'Christ, did you? It was one of the things I depended on as much as anything – when they took the privileges away it was that I hated most, I think, except perhaps not having books.' Almost without Quick's thinking, the association was there again – he and Jeremy had shared something which few others had shared and it was bound to make them want to talk; yet it was not true sharing – each was still, in his mind, concerned with what had been done to him. What had happened to the other mattered only as far as it was a reflection of what the self had experienced.

'I didn't mind those things at all,' said Jeremy. 'How long were you without?'

'Oh, four or five days – not long; but bad enough. And you? Were you allowed cigarettes and so on?'

'Oh, yes, I could have had them; I didn't, you may remember, lose any of my privileges.' The bitterness in his voice was such that for a moment Quick cursed himself for the tactlessness of the question – and then he grew angry that he should feel pity; why, it was one thing to try to understand, it was another to pity. Those who should really be pitied were Devis and Stevens – Jeremy did not deserve pity. Of course, Jeremy had cause to be bitter, Quick knew, for he had not fought his own disintegration – but he was his own cause; he was a prisoner of his own failure; those who had a right to bitterness were those whom Jeremy had sent to gaol.

All the same, his only reply was, 'No, of course, for a moment

I forgot'; and then they sat silent for a moment, each savouring the new situation in which each found himself. There was a small wind outside which came brushing the curtains behind Quick's head, which he could feel silkily on his cheek, which rustled the papers on the desk, which gently moved the cloth on the table, and which blew the hair back from Jeremy's forehead. Quick reached behind him and closed the window, as if he did not wish the wind to disturb this mood of his. It was not that Jeremy looked very different – whatever he had looked like when he came out of detention, he was now much as he had been before; there were no shadows under his eyes, no gauntness about the cheeks, no marring of the clear eyes – and whatever was new in him was not revealed in his way of holding himself. Perhaps, thought Quick, there is some new tension there, perhaps the holding is more self-conscious than it used to be; but that he knew might be his own reaction rather than Jeremy's. How hard it was to associate the man's action with the way he looked; it would be easier to come to terms with the action if you could see some decay in the body, some outward show of inward chaos. There was nothing there you could make the objective sign; it was all inside, it must be all inside, and he had to find it out. But he must wait; what came must come from Jeremy, not from him – he was not the supplicant.

Of course, it was Jeremy who moved first – he stood up and walked around the room, he went to the window, he opened the curtains, he looked out, he closed them again, he picked up a book from Henry's desk, he looked at its title, he put it down again, and he sat down. 'Well?' he asked Quick.

'That's my question, isn't it?' asked Quick. 'It's me who asks that; you are the one who answers.'

'All right,' said Jeremy. 'All right. What do you want me to answer?'

'I suppose in the first place, why you wanted to see me.'

Jeremy smiled. 'It's good to see that you at least haven't changed, Donald,' he said. 'Always straight to the heart of things – you don't like preliminaries much, do you?' He laughed suddenly, ironically. 'I remember once Mary telling me about you – she said that she wasn't even sure that you knew her name and then suddenly you came up to her and said, "I like you, you know," and then, about ten minutes later, "Will you come to bed with me, Mary?" She said that she was so surprised that she said yes almost before she had realized what you were asking.'

Quick did not laugh. 'She shouldn't have told you that, even if it is true,' he said.

'Sorry,' said Jeremy.'I am assuming too much again, am I?'

Again their conversation collapsed. It's an impossible situation, thought Quick – judging by his last remark, Jeremy had been hoping to renew their friendship as if it had not lapsed while he, interested simply in what had been in Jeremy that he had not seen before, wanted to keep them apart, wanted to talk as they had once been able to talk but without any of the old links. It was not going to work, he was sure; he was going to have to be content with not knowing. 'Look,' he said, 'I can't stay long – Mary is waiting at the party for me and I want to be there again within an hour.'

'Sorry, Donald – it's not easy to answer a question like that.'

'It should be – why did you want to see me? You must have known why when you asked Henry to arrange it.'

Jeremy did not reply; he got up from his chair again and walked over to the glass door which led out to the small verandah. He tried to open it but it was locked. He looked down to see if the key was in the lock; when he saw that it was not, he shook the door as if shaking would unlock it.

'Don't do that,' said Quick. 'It's locked and Henry has lost the key.'

'How do you get out there?'

'We climb out through the bedroom window – but Henry doesn't use it much except in the summer. I'll have to get another key, I suppose.'

'Good old Henry – do you know the story about how he lost the back door key when the police came and so couldn't let them in, when Devis was arrested, I mean?' said Jeremy.

'Yes, of course I know it. How do you know about it, Jeremy?'

'Oh, someone told me. I forget who. It's a lovely story, isn't it?'

'Yes,' said Quick and then, impatiently, 'Oh, for Christ's sake, Jeremy, we can't go on talking like this – you must tell me why you wanted to see me.'

Jeremy stood with his back to the door leading to the verandah. 'Don't you know yet?' he said. 'Surely you know, Donald?'

'No, I don't. I don't know anything; I don't know even why you turned state evidence and I don't know why you want to see me.'

'The two things don't necessarily have anything to do with each other.'

'For you they may not have – for me they have. I want to know why you turned state evidence, why you sent the others to gaol, and I want to know why you wanted to see me again.'

'Didn't you want to see me?'

'No, I didn't. I wish that I hadn't said I would. I want to understand why you did what you did and I thought that if I saw you I would understand. But I don't understand, I don't, and you don't seem ready to tell me.'

'Don't I?' Jeremy was doing his best to sound relaxed and amused, trying hard not to sound like Quick.

'Dammit, man, you won't even tell me why you wanted to see me. You must answer that, you must – otherwise I'm going away.'

Jeremy looked around the room; 'I can't tell you here,' he said; 'Let's go for a walk along the avenue. I'll try to tell you then.' He started to move towards the door of the flat but when Quick did not get up he stopped. 'Are you coming, Donald?' he asked.

'I don't think that I want to hear any more,' Quick said. 'I think I want you to go away from me. I don't think that you can tell me anything now.'

'I can – you'll know that when I've said what I've got to say.' Jeremy's voice was flat, cold, authoritative, exactly the voice of the old Jeremy; and Quick, even now, could not help marvelling at the self-assurance that was still in everything Jeremy did. How on earth does he manage, thought Quick, to keep the very heart of him from his eyes. He is a traitor and he must be hated. But, though Quick could say easily enough that he hated someone or something, he was not really very good at hatred and, almost involuntarily, he got up; that alone was enough to show Jeremy how close Quick was to breaking, how easy it would be to make him listen.

'All right,' said Quick. 'All right, I'll walk with you for exactly an hour and no longer.' He looked at his watch. 'Then I am going back to the party and you will have to go away.'

'An hour will be more than enough,' said Jeremy. 'But, really, I can't talk here. Let's go walking and I'll tell you then what I have to say.'

Outside, it was warm and very nearly still; the small wind came only occasionally from the sea and across the suburbs; the sky was overcast so there was no light except from the street-lamps. As they paused at the entrance to the blocks of flats before they turned to walk up the avenue that led along the railway line and then over it towards the sea, Jeremy pointed up; 'Look,' he said. 'You can just see the line of the mountain against the sky – it looks almost like a cloud, doesn't it?'

'I can't see it,' said Quick.

'I can,' said Jeremy. 'Do you remember that time when you gave me a lift, when we came through the mountains in winter?'

Quick hesitated – he did not want to make any gesture towards renewing their friendship; but he remembered too well to lie. 'Yes,' he said, 'I do remember.'

'Do you know, it's more than four years ago now? It doesn't feel like it.'

'It does to me,' said Quick. Jeremy did not seem to hear what he said; he seemed to have gone away somewhere inside himself, somewhere so far inside his mind that Quick could not follow him there.

'You know,' Jeremy went on, 'when I was inside, the one thing that I really wanted to see again was Table Mountain; you get so used to it when you live in the Cape, it makes you know that you're really here.' He laughed, almost as if he were remembering something amusing. 'Sometimes I used to think that the cell was nothing but a ship and that I wasn't in Cape Town at all; it was a ship and I was going out to sea; I suppose that's why I needed the mountain. Did you find that?'

'No,' said Quick, not prepared to share anything that he did not have to. 'No, all I wanted was cigarettes and books.'

'Oh,' said Jeremy. He began to walk up towards the avenue. Quick waited for a moment or two, then followed. 'Come on, Jeremy,' he said as he caught him up. 'You'd better talk quickly if you've anything but reminiscences.'

'All right,' said Jeremy. 'All right, I'll tell you. You want to know why I asked to see you?'

'Yes, of course,' said Quick. Jeremy stopped; he was in the shadow of a hedge and Quick, stopped a few paces further on, could not see for a moment where he was. He moved back a step and, as he did so, Jeremy moved out of the shadow – it seemed to Quick almost that a part of the shadow had detached itself and was moving towards him. Involuntarily he caught his breath; the moving shadow had frightened him. But it was only a moment of fear – then he was back in himself, impatient, aggrieved, wanting to walk fast now that he was out, not content to stop whenever Jeremy wanted to. 'Come on, Jeremy,' said Quick. 'If you want to think on your feet let's at least walk properly.'

'All right, I'll tell you,' said Jeremy. 'It's simple really – that's why I thought you'd have guessed; I wanted to see you because I still think of you as my friend.'

Quick nearly laughed out loud – it was so ludicrous to him that Jeremy should even suppose that such a thing was possible; it was ludicrous to him that this was what Jeremy should have been saving up. He deliberately made his answer as brutal as he could: 'Don't be silly, Jeremy. You can think that as much as you want. It's not enough of a reason, not for me anyway.' Yet he knew that this was really something to be afraid of, something that he had most feared might be what Jeremy wanted from him – he could not afford to be friends with Jeremy any more, he had to be his enemy, he had to hate him.

'Don't you count yourself as a friend of mine any more?' said Jeremy. They were walking again now, walking fast up the avenue towards the hill which bumped up just before the railway line.

'No,' said Quick, almost casually, 'No, I don't count traitors as my friends.'

'Are you sure that I'm a traitor?'

'If you aren't a traitor, what are you?'

'Oh, I'm a traitor all right,' said Jeremy – the speed which Quick was insisting on holding forced him to catch his breath. 'There's not much point pretending that I'm not. But you have to try to understand why.'

Now Quick stopped; 'Why do I have to understand?' he shouted. 'It's not "have" at all – I don't have to understand. Why should I?' He knew that Jeremy was right; he did have to understand, there was compulsion in it, but he could not bear that Jeremy should compel him to understand.

'Walk, man,' said Jeremy and, when Quick had caught up the few paces, he said, so quietly that Quick could hardly hear, 'because you are my friend.'

Again Quick stopped, again he shouted, 'Dammit, Jeremy, stop saying that – I was your friend once, I am not now. I will not be your friend.' But even as he said that he knew that, as long as he saw Jeremy, he could not help being his friend; there was too much between them to avoid the charge of friendship. Quick hated that, he hated that the new circumstances did not change the old.

'All right,' said Jeremy, 'you are not my friend any more – but you still have to understand why I turned state evidence, don't you? Don't you?' The question was asked not with any sense of pleading but with self-assurance; it was almost as if Jeremy was as sure of the wrong he had done as, before, he had been sure of the rightfulness of his beliefs.

Quick did not answer so Jeremy went on, 'Look, Donald, you don't understand, do you? You don't understand what happened to me, do you?' There was still no answer from Quick and suddenly he turned away from Jeremy and started to walk again, walking faster now as if he hoped to get away from Jeremy, almost as if he was being pursued by something, as a child in a dark street will walk faster and faster, not daring to run, until he can bear it no longer and will stop to give the beast on his tail a chance to spring. So, now, suddenly, Quick stopped. Jeremy reached out, caught his arm, and almost forced him around. 'Listen to me, Donald, you don't know, do you?'

Quick tore his arm away from Jeremy's grasp. 'Leave me alone,' he cried out. 'Don't touch me. No, I don't know – isn't it enough that you are a traitor, isn't it enough that you sent them to gaol? Why should I have to understand anything else?'

They were standing still, near the top of the hill, above the railway line that crossed the avenue. 'Poor transparent Donald,' said Jeremy. 'You want to understand, don't you? You really want to know why. And you can't work it out for yourself, can you? You with your logical mind want to see all the reasons laid out neatly in a pattern. And you can't see the pattern and you think that I may be able to find it for you. That's it, isn't it?'

'Yes,' said Quick and now he was pleading, even in that one word he was pleading. He could no longer bear his own stupidity. It was that note which Jeremy had been waiting for; but now it seemed almost that he could not answer.

'Oh my God, Donald. How can I of all people explain?'

'You must,' Quick said. 'Please, Jeremy, try to explain.'

'And if I tell you I can't explain, that I don't understand what happened to me, will you understand?' Jeremy stood close to Quick now, right in front of him, and though Quick and he were both accustomed to the dark now, though there was a streetlamp not far down the road from them, neither could see the other's face properly. 'I'll tell you what I do know, Donald. The moment that the police knocked on the door, they were bound to get me – and I knew even then that I would do anything to avoid going to gaol. Anything, no matter how foul it was; nothing that they could have done to me would have made any difference. It was there from the start. You know, Donald, I even moved those papers out from their hiding-place so that they would find them. I did it deliberately, I wanted the police to find them.'

'But why? Why? That's what I can't understand.'

Jeremy was crying now, standing still on the edge of the circled light of a street lamp. He brought his hands up to his face and, very slowly, rubbed them upwards almost as if there was another face over his own which he was trying to tear off. 'Because I am the man I am,' he said. 'Can't you understand that,

Donald? I've been a traitor inside me from the moment I was born. It's always been there, from the first day of my life. It's always been there, waiting to come out.'

'That's not true,' said Quick. 'You weren't a traitor before, we would all have trusted you with anything, with our lives.'

'That's because you can't understand. Oh, Donald, can't you see? I'm a special person – I'm not like the rest of you, I'm not like Hunter or the others. I'm separate, I'm my own self.'

Suddenly, for just a moment, Quick did understand; it was as though a sudden puff of wind had caught the defined edge of the street light and thrown it upwards like a net, thrown it right over Jeremy and himself. He saw what he had known about Jeremy from the start, he saw the enormous egocentricity which went with an equal distrust of self, a distrust of the privately heroic, a distrust which could only go with an egocentricity so certain that it could not be doubted – for if the self was the centre of the world, the touchstone of all judgements, the heart of light, then you could distrust it because it could not be destroyed. Quick saw, for just that one moment, that Jeremy had not broken, that Jeremy had not turned into anything – all he had done was to fulfil himself; he had said, I'm special, so it doesn't matter about the rest; whatever I believe outside me is not as important as this inside me – it may look wrong, it may even be wrong by all the objective codes, but I am preserving myself, I am making myself what I should really be.

But it was only for a moment that he saw it ; almost before he could imagine it, certainly before he could catch it and realize it in words, it had gone. All that he had left was a certainty that in some way Jeremy had not yet finished his explanation; there was something else, there was something Jeremy had not said, something he had to know. 'Jeremy, Jeremy, listen to me,' he said. 'What about me? Aren't I like you?'

As he asked that question he knew the answer; he was like Jeremy, he was exactly the same kind of person – he had that same egocentricity, that same urgent drive always towards his own centre – that was why they had been friends, that was why they had not been able to be complete friends, that was the shifting sand which had sometimes seemed to lie between them and which had sometimes seemed their friendship itself. But Quick could not bear that; the idea that he might be the same as Jeremy filled him with such horror that he took the idea and forced it away from his mind and, before Jeremy had a chance to answer, he cried out again, 'No, that isn't true. I wouldn't betray you. I'm not like you, I'm not a traitor.' And then suddenly he was crying too, standing just outside the circle of light, looking through the darkness at Jeremy's face. 'Oh, my God, Jeremy,' he said. 'What are we going to do?' The two of them stood, in a nearly dark street, so dark that they could hardly see each other, not daring to reach out to touch each other, and they were brothers in that and in everything. They belonged to each other, they shared the treachery, they shared everything, they were brothers.

It was only for a moment or two, it was not a continual sharing. It could not last – when they had met, it had been in beauty and that experience could not last, because it was, to each of them, a private experience that the other shared only by being there; now, when they shared anything properly for the first time, they both stood in terror at what they saw in themselves – and if Quick had been able to stand that terror, he would have gone on with Jeremy; but he could not. Jeremy at least went on.

Quick was in control of himself again before Jeremy. He moved a few yards away, a decent interval, to give Jeremy the chance to stop crying and, when he saw that Jeremy was all right again, he called out, 'Come on, Jeremy, I must get back.' He waited until Jeremy had crossed over to where he was waiting under the streetlamp and was about to start walking home again when Jeremy stopped him.

'Just a minute, Donald. I haven't finished yet,' he said.

'What do you mean?' said Quick. 'We can't go much further than we've gone already.'

'We can, you know. You asked the question yourself – what are we going to do now?'

Quick stood quite still; he looked almost as if Jeremy had spoken to him in some language he had never heard before. 'What do you mean?' he asked again.

'We can't just leave it like this – we've got to do something; you've got to help me, Donald.'

'Help you do what?'

'Help me make up for the treachery.'

Quick was certain that nothing could help; what they had seen – and already he had the feeling that what he had seen was disappearing – had been too important for anything at all to be done about it. 'There is nothing you can do about it now, Jeremy,' he said, 'except leave. You must go to some other country where you can learn to live with what you've done.'

Jeremy's self-assurance was coming back, for now he smiled at Quick. 'That won't do. You sound just like the judge did; and I'm not leaving. I'm going to stay and I'm going to show everyone that whatever I may have done my ideas haven't changed.'

'What are you going to do?'

'I know what I'm going to do – what I need to know is whether you'll help me. That's really what I wanted to find out tonight; are you still committed?'

'What are you going to do?' Quick repeated – he could not stand the easy way in which Jeremy used words like 'committed'; but he needed to know what Jeremy was thinking of.

As if to reply, Jeremy took his arm and gently turned him round so that they faced the sea again; then he began to walk again and, after a moment's hesitation, Quick came with him. Once they were out of the street light again, Jeremy said, 'I had a letter from Hunter a couple of months ago.'

'That surprises me,' said Quick. 'Where was it addressed from?'

'I don't know – it wasn't addressed. His girl-friend, you know that art-student, Patricia, she brought it to me and said that Hunter had sent it to her for me; she didn't know what it said.'

'What did Hunter say?' Quick was very suspicious; it seemed strange to him that Hunter should have written to Jeremy of all people, he was always suspicious of Hunter, and there was something in the tone of Jeremy's voice which disturbed him again.

'He said nothing at all about my being a traitor, not a word – I had expected it to be a very bitter letter but it wasn't at all. All it said was that he had made a separate cache of explosives which he didn't tell any of us about and that he thought I might be able to make use of it.'

'He's lying,' said Quick. 'He must be lying.'

'No, he's not – I've been to look and there is a cache where he said; he must have done it months ago.'

'Where is it?' asked Quick.

'I can't tell you that, Donald. But I am going to use it – will you help me?'

'Don't be a fool, Jeremy. You can't. How can you? The police will get you immediately.'

'No, why should they? They think that they've smashed me completely – they'll assume that it is a completely new group starting up.'

'Nonsense, Jeremy. But, tell me, how do you plan to use them?' Quick was so certain that this was a wild fling of Jeremy's imagination that he was being sarcastic – and when, a few moments later, he realized that it was possible that Jeremy was being completely serious, that he might really intend to use this secret cache of Hunter's to rehabilitate himself to himself, he had to reach out to touch the iron of a lamp-post to assure himself that this was really happening.

The plan was simple, Jeremy said – 'ludicrously simple', Quick muttered as he heard it. He wanted to fill an ordinary kit-bag, the kind that all South African rugby-players use, with as much plastic explosive and dynamite as it would hold, damp it down with a towel, and lead through the towel a fuse wire which he would connect to a converted alarm clock lying on the towel, with the alarm mechanism set to blow the fuse after five minutes – on top of the bag, to cover the alarm clock, he'd put a rugby jersey. That was the joke, he explained; the police would never think of searching a kit-bag full of games kit – and as he told Quick this, he giggled as any child might who planned to empty his father's whisky bottle and refill it with coloured water. But then he grew serious again; it was a foolproof plan, he explained. He would take the bag with him when he went to make his weekly report to the police, would stand it just behind the customer's side of the charge office counter, and would then leave without it. Exactly two minutes after Jeremy had left the charge office, Quick was to phone, warn the police that a bomb had been planted in the charge office, and tell them that they must clear the office immediately. A fuse set for five minutes would give the police time to clear the office but not time to search for the bomb or to dismantle it – anyway, they would not look in the kit-bag and provided the office was cleared there would be no danger to life, for the explosion would do no more than damage the one room – the police upstairs and the prisoners who might be in the cells would at most be shaken by the explosion.

'But don't you see how ludicrous it is?' Quick asked. 'Neither of us would have a chance even if the plan worked. The police know the connection between us, they'll know that you left the bag, they'll have both of us within an hour.'

'No,' said Jeremy. 'The bag will be utterly destroyed . . .'

'Oh, nonsense. Hunter told us that the police can trace explosives without any trouble – they'll be bound to connect it with the old work. And anyway, if you are serious about this plan, why do you need me? You could do it on your own.'

'I could, but I want you to help me – I want to be sure that nothing goes wrong.'

In Quick's mind the terrible suspicion was growing that Jeremy was trying in some way to trap him; he thrust the idea away from him – what he must do, he thought, is to show Jeremy how stupid it all is. 'Look,' he said, 'just think a minute. What happens if the police notice that you've left the kit-bag and make you take it?'

'Oh, I can disconnect the fuse without even taking the alarm out. I'll attach one of the wires so that I can pull it loose immediately I'm out of the police station, if necessary, though I'm sure it won't be.'

'And suppose they keep you longer than five minutes?'

'They never do. All I do is to put my head in at the door and the sergeant starts getting the report form ready on the desk for me to sign.'

'And how on earth would I be able to know that you've been delayed, if I've got to be phoning.'

'You can phone from the call box on the corner at the top of the street. I'll have to walk past there on my way to the bus and you'll be able to see whether or not I have the bag. It's a cinch, Donald, really it is – I've been over it again and again.'

'And how will you connect the fuse up inside the bag while you're in the office? Remember, you've got to set it for five minutes exactly.'

'Oh, I'll do that just before I go into the charge office. Anyone who saw me fiddling inside it will think that I'm just looking for something.'

'In the open street?' Gradually, Quick was being forced to see that Jeremy's plan could work, that, for all its ludicrous simplicity, it could be made to work – its simplicity was such that very little could go wrong. Now, he was being forced to look beyond the plan at the person who was planning it; now he was being forced to see where Jeremy was trying to lead him.

'Yes, Donald, right there. Or even inside the charge office. That's the best thing about the whole plan. Can't you see the beauty of it? The police think that they have cleared us out, that they have neutralized us, that we don't even have access to explosives, much less the desire to use them; now that Hunter's gone, they don't think even that we have the expertise to be dangerous. But they are wrong; we have explosives and Hunter taught me how to handle them.'

'As for Hunter,' said Quick, 'I think that he must be the most evil man I have ever met.'

'Why, Donald? Because he has given me a chance to make up for being a traitor?'

'Because he is trying to make you do something that he wouldn't have done himself.'

'Hunter wouldn't have become a traitor,' said Jeremy.

'Is that what you think?'

'Yes,' said Jeremy. 'Hunter's not like us, he's different – he's all the things that we are not – he's professional, committed, honest, and he believes in other people. He even believes in me still, which even you don't do.'

'Oh, don't fool yourself, Jeremy – Hunter's little more than a machine, a cold, calculating, inhuman bastard; he doesn't believe in you, he wants to use you.' Quick was sure of this; it seemed to him that Hunter had to take the responsibility as much as anyone

– but then he remembered that if Hunter had intended to use Jeremy, Jeremy in his turn now wanted to use him; that was what he had to fight. He was not going to let himself be made part of this insane plan; but how was he going to stop Jeremy? How could he persuade him? Was Jeremy even being serious? Was he not perhaps trying, after all, to trap him? Was this a new turn of treachery? Was Jeremy perhaps still working for the police? Was he trying to provoke a new outburst? Was that why the police had released him, so that they could put this madman on to him again?

'I won't have anything to do with your plan,' Quick said suddenly.

'Why not?'

'Because I think that it is futile, insane, ludicrous – either you are trying to fool me into something or else you are out of your mind.'

'Do you really think that I am that?' Jeremy sounded almost amused at the suggestion.

'Oh, for God's sake, I don't know. I reckon that anyone who can suggest such a plan as this must be unbalanced. A psychiatrist, that's what you need.'

Jeremy was close to him now, looking into his face; his shoulders were still set in the old half-pugnacious way; Quick looked hard back into the shadowy face. There was still such power in Jeremy's decisions, even if you were not sure that they were serious, that he was almost ready still to accept the plan. But he knew, he had to know, that anyone who could suggest such a scheme was mad; it was bloody ludicrous, the police would probably pick them both up before Jeremy had filled his kit-bag, and then it would be no good saying that he had not been prepared to get involved in the scheme. It would be no good saying that he had turned the scheme down. There was really only one way in which he could clear himself now, if Jeremy did intend the scheme – he would have to go to the police; and realizing that, he felt his rage at Jeremy rise again and under the rage always the suspicion that Jeremy knew what he was doing, that Jeremy was deliberately trying to make him go to the police, that Jeremy was trying to make him into a traitor too. Why else should he be pretending to plot another wave of sabotage? He could not intend it – this was a trap, either a trap set by the police or a trap which Jeremy was setting privately, a trap which Jeremy had worked out very carefully so that he could drag him down into his private hell. It was too late now; he was trapped; there was no way out now; he was caught just as he had been caught by Jeremy before.

Quick's gesture at Jeremy was faint, almost that of a man recovering from an illness. Stopped in the light of a street lamp, he said, 'Get away from me, Jeremy. Get away. I will have nothing to do with you and your insane schemes.' Jeremy did not move and he repeated it, 'Go away. I don't want you. Go away, damn you'; he was finding his voice now and the rage seemed to have gone – all that was left was his certainty that Jeremy was conspiring to destroy him, that Jeremy was part of a plot by all his enemies, that Jeremy was trying to drag him down into his private drowning. When Jeremy did not move, Quick himself turned away and started to walk back down the avenue towards the flat.

'Who's the traitor now, Quick?' Jeremy called after him and Quick stopped, turned, paused, then walked back, looking almost as if he was going to attack Jeremy. But he stopped himself a few yards off and said, 'You're the traitor, Jeremy – I was beginning to feel pity for you but I don't any more; you're still the only traitor and you won't make me a traitor. I'm finished with you and yours, do you hear? You can count me out from now on – I'm going to stop being your servant, I'm going to be myself.'

Jeremy was laughing, letting the full joke of whatever it was he saw ride into his face, and then he turned away from Quick and walked off up the avenue.

14

Quick went straight back to the party; he wanted only to see Mary, to talk to her, to tell her what Jeremy had done, to tell her how Jeremy had tried to trap him, to ask her what he should do. But when he got there she was gone.

'Where's Mary?' he asked Henry, dragging him away from the girl he was talking to.

'She was tired, so I drove her back to her room and then came back here. Did you see Jeremy? Did it go off all right?'

'It was terrible. I'll tell you later. I must go to Mary now,' Quick answered and left the party, running in his anxiety to be with Mary.

She was waiting for him but when he tried to kiss her she held him away. 'Tell me what happened, please, Donald. I have to know. I could not stand being at that idiotic party knowing that you were with Jeremy again.'

'It was terrible,' he said again. 'I think that he may be completely mad. He pretends to have this insane scheme of blowing something up with some explosives the police did not find – I tell you, he's either mad or he's working for the police still.'

As he said this, Mary turned away from him; she had seemed very excited when he came in but now that he said this her shoulders seemed to sag and her face to grow very tired. 'He told you about the plan to blow up the police station, did he? I told him that it was no use telling you,' she said. She looked at him very deliberately, almost coldly.

Quick, who had been prowling restlessly about the room, picking up books, looking at their titles, and then putting them down again, suddenly stopped and turned to her. 'You know about it?' he asked. 'How do you know about it? How?'

'Yes, I do know; Jeremy told me.'

'When did he tell you? When did you see him? Why didn't you tell me that you'd seen him?'

'How could I tell you when I knew how you felt about it all?'

'What exactly did he tell you?'

'I suppose the same that he told you – all about the kit-bag full of explosives, five minutes to wait, and all that.'

'That's it – and it's mad, isn't it? Or if he isn't mad, he's trying to trap us, either for himself or for the police.' For a moment Quick seemed to forget the puzzle about Mary's having seen Jeremy so that he could concentrate on the more immediate one of Jeremy's motives – she looked up to see if he was going to continue the inquisition and as she did he remembered and asked her, 'Where did you see him?'

'He told me the plan here.'

'Here? In your room? Did you throw him out?'

Mary shook her head.

'Why not? Can't you see that he's out of his mind? Either that or he's working for the police still.'

'I don't think so.'

'But, darling, can't you see? Don't you see how stupid the whole idea is? Jeremy's no longer reliable, something's smashed in him, he can't see the consequences of his own actions; you can't rely on him any more, you can't.'

'You relied on him for a long time, Donald.'

'That was before. He's a traitor now, darling; you've got to face that. Oh, I know that I still feel some of the old things about him too, but the basic thing has changed, really it's changed.'

'Not all that much.' Mary was sitting so low in her armchair that Quick could not see her face – he was still standing, looking across the room at her.

'All that much,' he contradicted her; but she did not reply and did not look at him. He moved a pace forward but he could still not see; her hair had fallen across her eyes and she did not brush it away – she seemed almost to be hiding in it.

'What are you going to do, Mary?' he asked.

'What I did before.'

'You didn't do anything before.'

'You don't know that, do you?'

Quick felt suddenly that he could no longer stand – for a moment he seemed to be moving towards Mary, as though he was going to sit on the arm of her chair, but then he almost fell into the high-backed chair at the desk. 'You'd better tell me what's going on, Mary,' he said. 'I seem to be getting a little lost again.'

'Do you really want to know?'

'Is it all that unpleasant? You'd better tell me.'

Mary looked up at him – she seemed to be on the point of smiling. 'Where do I start?' she said. 'Do you remember that night a few weeks ago when I came home early because I was tired?' Quick nodded – it was the night after which Mrs Jeremy had come to Henry's flat. Mary went on, 'Well, I wasn't tired. I wanted to get back here to see Jeremy. I wanted to get back here so that I could', and now she did smile, 'go to bed with him.' It was not at all a smile of malice, Quick could see; it was partly a smile of embarrassment, partly one of a kind of delight – and the smile, for a moment, seemed to take the sting out of what she had said.

'What? Good heavens.' Quick snorted. 'Didn't I satisfy you?'

'That's got nothing to do with it.'

'You were sleeping with Jeremy,' he said, as if saying it himself would make it easier to believe. 'When did this start?'

'Oh, a long time ago – long before you were arrested.'

'As long ago as that? Well, I'm surprised,' said Quick. He was doing his best to play the role of the worldly wise man, the kind of man who would, he thought, accept infidelity in his stride. 'Did Sheilagh know?' he asked.

'Yes, I think so.'

'Didn't she mind?'

'She didn't seem to.'

'But I thought that Jeremy was supposed to have asked her to marry him, after they were released. Didn't he?'

'He told me that he felt he ought to.'

'Oh nonsense.' He jumped up from his chair and began to move towards her again – but when she made no sign of having seen him he stopped. 'Good God, Mary, why? Why did it first happen?'

'Jeremy asked me to go to bed with him and I went.'

'Just like I did. So . . .' Quick began; but Mary interrupted him.

'No,' she said, 'Not at all like you did.'

'So,' Quick went on, as if he had not heard her, 'that bastard wasn't content to betray me, he had to cuckold me as well, and now he's trying to trap me with this plan of his.'

'He didn't betray you and he isn't trying to trap you – he's deadly serious about this plan, Donald.'

'He did betray me, you know; he betrayed me, you, Sheilagh, the whole bloody lot of us. Was he good in bed?'

'Oh, don't be silly. That didn't matter.'

'It matters that you went to bed with him. It makes you a true revolutionary, doesn't it? You sleep with a saboteur, it's as good as being a saboteur yourself. Well, I'm buggered. I never thought that. When did you last sleep with him?'

'It doesn't concern you.'

'It does – you sleep with me still, don't you? Have you ever slept with both of us on the same night?'

'Oh, don't, Donald. You don't understand at all.'

'I'm beginning to. When did you first sleep with him?'

'I can't remember.'

'Oh, nonsense, you must be able to remember.'

'All right, then, I'll tell you. It happened first just after you left the cottage.'

'I see. He wanted you to get back at me – really quite simple isn't it?'

'That wasn't the reason, Donald, and you know that wasn't the reason – you simply can't understand what I felt, what Jeremy felt.'

'I understand well enough,' said Quick. He stood up, not looking at Mary. 'Well, I suppose that I had better go. Would you mind posting any of my belongings to me? There may be some of my books.'

'I'm sorry, Donald.'

'Sorry! Christ, that's a little late, isn't it? Oh, there's no point getting bitter about it; I confess that I don't really understand all this. . . . I suppose I shall, one day.'

'Aren't you going to tell me what to do about this plan of Jeremy's?' For the first time since she had told him she looked straight at him again but now he avoided looking back at her. He wanted only to get out of this place, out of any place where Jeremy had been.

'Perhaps Jeremy will give you better advice himself,' Quick said. 'He seems to be pretty much a success all round.'

'Please, Donald, I don't know what to do.'

'All right, I'll tell you – go to the police and tell them Jeremy's plan.'

'Please be serious, Donald. What can I do?'

'I'm being dead serious. That is the only thing you can do. You've got a choice; you're for or you're against. Either you help him or you tell the police. If he means this plan, you won't persuade him he's wrong, you know.'

'I know. And I don't think I can do either of those things,' Mary said.

'Neither can I,' said Quick and he left her, leaving her still in the armchair.

It was very quiet outside. Quick, as he stood under the trees where he had parked his car, listened for any murmuring that might disturb the sleep of the lower air. The upper air, the air of the mountains, the air of the stars, is dancing, he thought; but around him there was no movement, no noise. The first heat of early summer lay against his skin like a second skin. Mary's hair, he remembered, had always fallen across her eyes; sometimes he would pretend to creep under it to hide – when she was awake she gave herself gladly, when she was asleep she turned away from him, arms tight across her breasts, legs curled up against her stomach. Oh, you had to choose all right; you were against or you were for. For people like him, who knew what had to be done but who were not sure that the doing would end where reason ended it, there wasn't a place left at all. There was only one way out, for if you made the right choice you died and who would choose death? That part of it was easy to see, though it didn't make the choice any easier; what was not so easy to see was why excitement, exhilaration, almost desire, yes, it was desire, still mocked what he should be feeling. Jeremy had slept with Mary all right; did it matter? Yes; but suddenly it seemed right and proper; it made the betrayal complete and to be complete was good.

Suddenly Quick turned away from his car and walked back to Mary's room. He wanted her and she would have him now; she would need him and he wanted her. All that was alive in the world called him back to her. But when he got to her door he stopped and listened; and he heard that she was talking to someone and realized that she must have phoned Jeremy as soon as he had left. Now if I wait, he thought, she'll go to him and I can follow; or else he will come to her and I can see. The rage began to blow through him, gust after gust, nausea, the shakes, the dancing air inside his head, the leaves bending and leaping, the great branches crashing from the trees.

15

Henry Naude was at the flat by the time Quick got back; he had had to stop several times on his way, once to be sick, twice because he could not see the road; but he did not go into Henry's room. He went straight into his own and began to pack up his cases and his books. After a few minutes, Henry came in. He looked a little drunk, his hair untidy, his face red, his shirt sweaty.

'Are you all right?' he asked Quick. There was no reply so he repeated his question; 'Donald, are you all right?'

'Yes, I'm all right.' He stood up and looked at Henry, then said, 'Perhaps I should ask you that question.'

'Oh, I'm all right, just a little drunk. I always seem to be drunk at times of crisis – I presume that this is a crisis, since you seem to be leaving the flat.'

'Yes, I'm going to stay at home for a bit. I'll go on paying my share of the rent until you find someone to move in with you.'

'Oh, that doesn't matter,' said Henry. 'I hope that your going isn't something to do with me.'

'No, not really. I do wish that you hadn't asked me to see Jeremy.'

'I'm sorry – I wrote to him after he was released to say that I'd help him if he needed help. He said he didn't want any then and then, about a week ago, he asked me to arrange for you two to meet. I thought I had to; I did ask him if I could. Perhaps it was a mistake.'

'No, it wasn't your fault. It had to happen sooner or later.'

'No, perhaps it was my fault. Do you know, Koos Reisman wrote to me when he left the country to say that he had been to see Jeremy; and he warned me to have nothing to do with him? I think that was why he left the country so suddenly, you know.'

Quick looked up. 'You didn't tell me that Koos wrote to you.'

'No. I thought it might upset you, Koos's letter, Koos having been to see Jeremy too.'

'Did he say anything about me?'

'Just sent his regards – all he said was that he had been to see Jeremy and that it was something I should avoid. It seems that I should have taken his advice.'

'Perhaps you should've. But it doesn't matter, really. It would have happened just the same, probably.'

'Can you tell me what happened, or don't you want to?'

'I can't tell you, Henry. I simply can't. I'm sorry.' But if Koos left the country after seeing Jeremy, it might be, he thought, that Jeremy tried the same plan on Koos; and if that's so, I don't blame Koos for running so far or so fast.

'Henry, do you know why I agreed to see Jeremy?' he asked suddenly.

'I don't know – I suppose it was because you felt that as one of his friends you owed him something.' For each of them, it was always his own reason he gave, even for someone else's action – Henry knew why he had helped Jeremy and so he assumed that everyone else who went near him did so for the same reason; it was a kind of selfishness but a different kind of selfishness than that which governed Quick's reactions to Jeremy, to Jeremy's plan, to Mary's love for Jeremy.

'No, it wasn't that,' said Quick. 'I wanted simply to know why he turned traitor; I couldn't understand and I wanted to know. And you know, I didn't find out – I found out other things, terrible things, but I didn't find that out.' He turned away from Henry and went on with his packing – but he knew that he was not telling the truth, even to himself; he was very near to telling himself the truth, he was near the point where he could look at Jeremy and himself to say, Yes, that's the crux of it. But having got that close to discovery, he found that he did not want to know – it was not that he was content to go no nearer, it was that he was unable to. He was like an explorer who had reached a new country, who knew that inside it there were rarities and treasures that no man had yet seen, and who found the shores too dangerous for a landing; he wanted to land, he had to land, but he could not – for he knew, perhaps not entirely consciously, but still he knew, that he was involved in Jeremy's treachery, as he would always be involved in it. If, on the one hand, he was not prepared to help Jeremy, on the other he was not prepared to go to the police; and perhaps he might have decided to help Jeremy, he thought, if he had not discovered about Jeremy and Mary – that was the cruellest throw that the gods had made; they had not been content to present him with a choice, they had presented it in such a way that he had no choice. Even now, Quick could not see that his choice was his own, that for someone else it would not have been a choice at all.

'Have you found out something about Mary?' Henry asked quietly – he did not seem to be very drunk any more.

Quick looked up from his packing. 'Yes, I did,' he said. 'I found out a lot about her. Why did you ask?'

'Because I wondered that you hadn't stayed there tonight.'

'Tell me, Henry,' Quick asked suddenly – he did not want to give himself time to think about what he was asking. 'Did you know that Mary was sleeping with Jeremy all the time that she was supposed to be with me?'

'Yes, I suppose I did. Oh, I wasn't sure, but I thought that she might be. I mean, I'm not surprised to hear that she was. Did Jeremy tell you that?'

'No, Mary did. Why didn't you tell me?'

'How could I tell you? You would have hated me too if I had told you.'

'I know. Thank you, Henry, thank you for not telling me.' Quick turned away again and asked, quietly, 'Do you think that a lot of people suspected that Mary was sleeping with Jeremy?' He had to ask that – had everyone been aware of what Jeremy was doing to him? Had his shame been obvious?

'I heard a few sarcastic remarks from people – but I don't think there was much talk about it.'

'I suppose that I should have guessed myself beforehand but, really, I didn't even suspect it. That's meant to be the trouble with things like that always: you see so clearly afterwards all the things that you should have seen before and you feel such a bloody fool not to have realized.'

'I wouldn't know,' said Henry. 'I've never stayed with one girl long enough to know things like that.' Then, very gently, he asked, 'Is that the only trouble?'

'Only you, Henry, could suggest that it was not enough of a trouble to have your girl sleep with the man you used to think was your best friend.' Quick tried to smile at him. 'But it isn't the only trouble – it's only the most immediate.'

'Is there anything I can do?'

'Tell me one thing – has Jeremy said anything to you about his plans?'

'No. He's said nothing, almost nothing, to me at all – I simply fetched him, drove him here, and left him to wait for you.'

'Well, thank goodness for that. If Jeremy tries to see you again, take my advice as well as Koos's and refuse to have anything to do with him. Don't even listen to him. He is very dangerous at the moment and he is a traitor.'

'He's not likely to talk to me, Donald. Don't you remember? I'm politically suspect; I've a father who is a Nationalist and Jeremy believes that the sons are responsible for their fathers – what I think doesn't matter to Jeremy; what matters is my name.'

'You hate him too, don't you, Henry? For that and for Arthur too, I suppose. Well, so do I, and he was my friend once, which makes me hate him even more now.'

Nothing more was said; and that same night, Quick left the flat and went to his parents' home. They were in bed when he got there but they got up, made a bed for him, and did not ask a single question. It was obvious from his face that there had been some trouble and they thought it best to take him in and to ask no questions until he told them what it was.

On the Monday morning Mrs Quick phoned the newspaper office to tell the editor that Quick was ill; and soon afterwards Quick himself wrote asking if he could go on indefinite sick leave, pending his resignation, since he intended to go overseas permanently in the near future. He saw neither Jeremy nor Mary;

and when Henry came to see him, Mrs Quick told him that Donald had said that he did not want to see anyone, not even Henry. Most people were given to understand that Quick had had some kind of breakdown. But it was not true; he was perfectly normal, both physically and mentally; he had simply decided that he was going to leave South Africa, as soon as he possibly could. For him, it seemed the only way out.

16

The rest of the story takes little telling. Three days before Quick was due to leave the country by boat for the United Kingdom, Jeremy carried out his plan. It worked almost as he had told Quick; he took his kit-bag loaded with explosives into the Caledon Square charge office when he went to make his weekly report, he stood it against the counter where he thought the sergeant on duty could not see it and, while the sergeant was getting the report form, he bent down and set the fuse as he had planned to, for five minutes. He had signed the report form, the sergeant had witnessed it, and he had left without the bag.

As soon as he got out of the charge office, he started off up the street to the phone box on the corner from which Mary was to make the call to warn the police to clear the office. When he had gone only about thirty yards up the street, the sergeant came out of the office carrying the bag and called up the street, 'Eh, Mr Jeremy, you forgot your kit-bag.' Jeremy stopped, turned, saw the sergeant with the kit-bag, hesitated for a moment, then turned and ran away up the street. He did not stop even for Mary, waiting in the call box. Nobody knew whether his nerve broke or whether he simply wanted his plan to succeed somehow. The sergeant had not run after him but had stood outside the charge office, on the pavement, and had, after a moment or two, put the kit-bag down. Again, nobody knew whether Jeremy had set the fuse for less than five minutes, either by chance or on purpose, or whether the sergeant's putting the bag down set the fuse off early.

The explosion killed the sergeant and two passers-by, a woman and her son, and injured seven others – it was in the middle of an afternoon and the pavement was not crowded. Jeremy was arrested an hour later, at his home; the police found him, they said at his trial, lying on his bed, waiting for them. Mary the police arrested later that night, when she gave herself up at the Wynberg police station; Henry Naude, who drove her to the police station, was arrested too and so was Quick, from his parents' home while they were having dinner.

Henry was held for twenty-four hours only and was then released; Quick was held for five days more, long enough for him to miss his passage to England, but he was then released. Once the police had told him about the explosion, he had told them immediately all that he knew; although there was much awkwardness about the cache of explosives which the police thought Quick must have known more about than he could tell, the fact that Jeremy insisted that Quick had tried to dissuade him and the fact that Quick's hatred of violence was already established made the police sure that he was really clean – and Quick did not hesitate to tell the police that he thought that Jeremy's plan had been nothing but insane imagination; he had not, he insisted, thought that any sane man could have intended it seriously. It was Quick's insistence that Jeremy must be insane which made the police decide not to use him as a state witness; they wanted Jeremy to take full responsibility for what he had done, they would not let him escape with an excuse of insanity.

Quick left South Africa, on an exit permit, within two weeks of being released and before Jeremy and Mary were brought to trial. They were charged jointly with murder and were then remanded for a week to allow their defending lawyers to consult psychiatrists; State psychiatrists had already examined both of them and had decided that they were fit to plead. At the start of the trial, Mary's defence pleaded successfully for a separation of trials – and she was tried on a charge of murder before a Judge and two assessors in the High Court in Cape Town, convicted though with extenuating circumstances, and so sentenced to only ten years' imprisonment.

Jeremy's trial was even shorter; his lawyers argued, without much conviction as it seemed, that he had been temporarily insane – they even managed to get a university psychology teacher to give evidence of his mental instability; the judge treated the evidence very roughly. Nobody thought that Jeremy was insane. His lawyers tried too to argue mitigation, pleading his youth, his political beliefs, his despair at having given evidence at the trial of Stevens and Devis, his family background; but the judge sentenced him to death and nobody was much surprised. He was executed on the morning of 15 April 1965.

Epilogue

In some ways, it had all happened a long time ago, or so it seemed to Quick. When he had arrived in England, he had worked for a year on a small provincial newspaper in the north of England. Then he had been offered a special scholarship for older students at his father's old college; he had accepted it and, after a year, had met an English girl whom he had married as soon as he could; after a year they had a daughter whom Quick had insisted on calling Rosaline – in his exile he had begun to cultivate irony and he wanted his daughter to be named after the Rosaline of *Love's Labour Lost*, though he did not tell his wife that. Like his wife, Rosaline was very beautiful and very silent and Quick loved them both very much; and was incomplete.

Sometimes he would see other South African exiles – Henry Naude came on a visit to England and spent a week-end with Quick in Oxford; Koos Reisman called in for tea one Sunday afternoon; and Raymond Roseman and his wife were among the four or five South Africans invited to the party which Quick and his wife gave after their wedding. Hunter, who was most of the time in Africa training revolutionary soldiers, came to London occasionally and once wrote to Quick suggesting that they meet; but Quick tore up the letter.

Pacifist, exile, modern, obscure, he sat each day in a library in Oxford; and was incomplete. Since its self-conscious ironies suited his new manner, he loved Oxford too – a centre of scholarship, the doors of which opened on to London, old habits, old-fashioned habits, and an industrial town beating about the ears of the university. There he was no one, except to his wife and perhaps to his child; that pleased him, that 'perhaps' pleased him especially. And Africa still perched over his heart, a great beautiful beast of wings and claws; and he was content that it should stay there.

Sometimes it seemed to him that a man was only completely a man when he was dead; as Jeremy was to him completely a man, traitor and hero, even though his heart had been eaten. Just before he was executed, Jeremy had written to him in England. 'I wanted to write to you,' he wrote, 'to say that I hope that you do not still hate me. I think often of our first meeting – do you remember those mountains? There don't seem to be any left for me now, perhaps just this last little hill which doesn't take much climbing or much appreciation. In some ways I am content to die – but don't take that to mean that I am dying content – there is too much that I wish I could have done. But no one will be able to think of me as a hero, thank God, so I hope that all of you, you especially, now that you have, as I hear, left for good, will not try to remember me. I don't really expect to be forgiven, in a way I don't want to be, but I do hope that you won't still hate me. I hope that you will be happy.' That was all.

But he had not exorcized Quick's ghosts; and every evening, when the time came for him to leave the library for his home, Quick would look up into the still air for all their faces, the faces of his friends and the faces of the dead – and always they would merge into that one face, laughing and in despair, Jeremy's face when he had last seen him. Quick would stand on the steps of the library and look up to the windows of the rooms he worked in, as if he hoped that Jeremy would look down from the same windows so that he could ask him again what had happened. The light was all around him, all the knowledge that a man could need; and he did not know; and he could not forget.

More about Penguins

Penguinews, which appears every month, contains details of all the new books issued by Penguins as they are published. From time to time it is supplemented by *Penguins in Print*, which is a complete list of all books published by Penguins which are in print. (There are well over three thousand of these.)

A specimen copy of *Penguinews* will be sent to you free on request, and you can become a subscriber for the price of the postage. For a year's issues (including the complete lists) please send 30p if you live in the United Kingdom, or 60p if you live elsewhere. Just write to Dept EP, Penguin Books Ltd, Harmondsworth, Middlesex, enclosing a cheque or postal order, and your name will be added to the mailing list.

Some other Penguins by South African writers are described on the following pages.

Note: *Penguinews* and *Penguins in Print* are not available in the U.S.A. or Canada

The Keep

Jillian Becker

'Mrs Foster expelled Simon because he is disobedient, retarded and bloody-minded . . . and Nanny has spoilt him and excused him and let him get away with – well – murder!'

Johannesburg, the 1930s. Two children – clever, plain Josephine and backward, destructive Simon – grow up over-indulged by their cockney Nanny; neglected by their parents: Rayfel, a rhetorical lawyer preoccupied with politics, and Freda, a cultured heiress scornful of Johannesburg society.

The Keep is a perfectly focused study of a family at cross-purposes under a bland veneer of conventions; of characters incapable of facing domestic or political realities. In it, pre-war South African bourgeois life becomes almost palpable – with people, places, sights and smells rising off the page to hold you rapt, astounded and horrified.

Too Late the Phalarope

Alan Paton

'So we drove back to Venterspan when the sun was almost down, and the world was full and the world was filled with beauty and terror. And darkness came over the grass country, and over the continent of Africa, and over man's home and the earth, and over us all. And the sun went down, and never rose again.'

Alan Paton's second novel is more than a story of sexual temptation; more than a story of South Africa's tragic racial problems; it is a tragic masterpiece, a worthy successor to his famous first novel, *Cry, the Beloved Country*.

Also available

Cry the Beloved Country

Debbie Go Home

Not for sale in the U.S.A. or Canada